CRY OF THE LOON

Sally DeFreitas

Sally DeFreitas

PublishAmerica
Baltimore

PublishAmerica has allowed this work to remain exactly as the author intended, verbatim, without editorial input.

Softcover 9781629075419
PUBLISHED BY PUBLISHAMERICA, LLLP
www.publishamerica.com
Baltimore

Printed in the United States of America

CHAPTER ONE

"Frank, what was that?"

"What was what?"

"That," I said as a mournful cry echoed through the trees. The eerie, haunting sound sent a chill up my spine, despite the warm spring weather.

"It's a loon, silly." Frank shook his head as though appalled at my ignorance. "Haven't you ever heard one before?"

"Hey, I'm a city girl."

Frank smiled at me, an endearing smile that revealed the gap between his two front teeth. "Well, now you know what a loon sounds like. No surprise since we are only a couple of miles from Loon Lake. The sad part is, that cry of the loon is becoming rare. They seem to be fast disappearing." Frank, the outdoorsman, was always slipping in little lectures on the environment.

"Okay, now I know what a loon sounds like. But I have yet to figure out what a morel looks like—in its natural habitat, that is."

"Don't worry, you'll get the hang of it."

This was Frank Kolowsky trying to be encouraging. Usually this mode just irritated me—as did some of his other habits. Even so, we had managed some semblance of a relationship for close to a year— probably because we are both transplants to a West Michigan village that offers a limited choice of romantic partners.

"How am I supposed to see something brown and wrinkled," I said, "when it's hiding under brown, wrinkled leaves?" After an hour without success, I was feeling frustrated. "And why should I care, anyway?"

"Come on, it's a new experience. The morel is a delicacy that refuses to be cultivated. The only way to find a morel is to go out and look for it."

That's why we were tramping through the Manistee National Forest, just two days after a warm rain that Frank had said was sure to bring out the elusive fungi. And he was right about that, but so far the score was twenty for Frank and a big fat zero for me. This I also found irritating.

I took a deep breath, inhaling the yeasty scent of damp leaves and moss. We resumed a slow walk—scanning the ground in front of us and making detours around trees. "How come you find these things but I can't?"

"Maybe it's because I'm a detective."

"Don't give me that," I said with an unladylike snort. "My eyes are as good as yours. There must be a trick you haven't told me about."

"Maybe it's because you're a city girl."

"I don't buy that either. Didn't you grow up in Detroit?"

"I did. But my mom's parents still had the family farm. And every May, we spent a Sunday in the woods looking for morels. Kind of made a picnic out of it." He stopped and made a beckoning motion. "Okay now, come on over here."

I sighed as I went over and stood next to him. "Now what?"

"Just look," he said, pointing to a patch of ground that looked exactly like the rest of the forest floor.

"I'm looking. What's the big deal?"

"Okay now. Crouch down a little. And look where I'm pointing."

I crouched. I looked. I still don't see anything.

"You're looking for a break in the leaves. Or a little hump where something is poking through."

"I see it!" I squealed with delight and lunged forward to pick my very first morel.

Seconds later, I heard the cry of the loon again and a dark cloud drifted over the sun. But nothing could dampen my spirits over the next hour as I continued to find and pick morels.

Frank was getting two for every one of mine but that didn't bother me because I was finally caught up in the spirit of the search. I greeted each discovery with a triumphant cry, then carefully broke off the pale stem and put the crinkled mushroom in my net bag. Frank had provided onion bags for the occasion, explaining that they allowed the harvested morels to scatter spores that would become the crop for another spring.

My mood was improving by the minute. The clouds came and went but offered no rain. Squirrels scolded us from the safety of their hiding places.

"Hey, this is fun," I said. "Maybe I won't move back to Chicago after all."

"Were you really thinking about it?"

"Didn't you hear me moaning all winter about our isolation, the lack of diversion and my utter boredom with Shagoni River?"

"A lot of people do that."

"Even you, as I recall."

"Of course. But it's just a way of letting off steam. Then comes spring and we're all thrilled to be living in a lovely village on the shore of Lake Michigan."

"It is pretty nice."

"Besides, you have me."

I swallowed a number of retorts as I bent to pluck a large fist shaped mushroom and placed it carefully in my bag. I scanned the surrounding area but failed to see another, and finally gave in to the ache in my back.

"I'm ready for a break," I said as I stood straight, put both hands on my lumbar area and arched my spine. I was afraid Frank would resist the suggestion and call me a wimp, but for once he agreed.

"Guess I'm ready too," he said. "I think it's time for a picnic."

"Really? You brought food?" I eyed the khaki vest he was wearing, with its multitude of compartments and pockets. I realized that I was hungry as well as tired. Breakfast had been hours ago.

"Right here." He reached into one of his pockets and produced a pair of granola bars.

"Thank heaven," I said as he handed me one. "I hope they have lots of chocolate."

"I hope so too. But if not,"—he reached into another pocket and pulled out a generous bag of trail mix—"I'm sure this does."

"Great—but I'll still starve if I can't get this open." I struggled with the wrapping on the granola bar and finally started tearing at it with my teeth.

"I'll open that for you," Frank said as he produced a pocketknife, "but let's be civilized and sit down."

I eyed the ground warily. "I'm not eager for a wet butt."

"No problem. You can sit on my vest."

"Okay. But what about you?"

"Maybe we can share."

"Sounds like a plan."

Minutes later we had picked out a spot that was level and relatively dry. Frank put his vest on the ground, spread it out, and we found there was room for both of us, provided we scrunched together. We placed our mushroom bags on the ground beside us.

Frank opened the granola bars and I lost no time dispatching mine—the fresh air had given me a lumberman's appetite. As we shared the bag of trail mix, which included plenty of chocolate, Frank talked about cooking the morels.

"We might as well have them for supper tonight. I'll dredge them in flour and fry them in butter."

"I don't think I have any butter—can we use margarine?"

"No way. It has to be butter."

Sometimes Frank is pretty inflexible. "Okay. If I don't have butter at home, we can probably borrow some from Les and Daisy." Les and Daisy were our newlywed neighbors—senior citizen newlyweds.

"How are they doing?" he said. "I haven't seen them since their wedding."

"Les and Daisy were smart. After their honeymoon cruise they spent a month with her niece in Florida and came home about the first of April. I knew when they got back because Les came over to shovel my porch and Daisy sent over some chocolate chip cookies."

"Lucky girl. I don't recall that you shared them with me."

"That's because you were out of town."

We were sitting pretty much back to back now, lending each other support. "Why are you wiggling around like that?" he said.

"Because I'm sitting on something—."

"You're sitting on my vest—and I definitely took all the hardware out of it."

"Maybe you missed something. It feels really hard."

"Aren't you delicate—like the princess and the pea."

"Well it's more than a pea."

"Just ignore it."

This was typical Frank. He was always the kind of guy to tough things out—another irritating trait of his. I was not about to tough this out. I handed him the package of trail mix, shifted to a kneeling position and scooted away from the place I'd been sitting. I examined the vest but didn't find anything in it that might have caused my discomfort. So I folded it back to examine the ground underneath.

Now I could feel the offending object. It was partially buried.

"See, there is something here," I said.

"Probably the root of a tree."

"Well maybe." I started to dig the leaves and dirt away from the thing I had been sitting on. My fingers touched a protuberance that felt like bone. I drew my hand away. "Frank, check this out. I think it might be a bone."

"Probably just some animal." He knelt down, folded back the cloth and continued to paw the dirt at my excavation spot.

I retrieved the trail mix, stood up and fed myself a handful. I was just going for another serving when I heard him say, "Good lord."

"So what is it?"

"It's a bone. I'm pretty sure it's a finger bone."

"A finger. Umm—like a human finger?"

"Yes. I think we're the only animal with digits like this."

"Oh cripe." As he continued to dig, I backed away and dropped all of the trail mix. My appetite was gone.

"Looks like we've got ourselves a hand here."

"A hand?"

"That's right. At least it used to be—a human hand."

The haunting cry of the loon echoed through the forest once again.

CHAPTER TWO

The spring day, with all of the chattering squirrels and birdsong, no longer felt idyllic. The discovery of human remains left me feeling totally creeped out with a desire to be far away from the place as soon as possible. I stood at a distance while Frank continued to dig.

After a few minutes he stopped. "I'm not going to dig any more," he said. "It's clear that the hand is fastened to something else and my best guess is that it's a wrist and then an arm and—."

"You mean a whole body?"

"Can't tell for sure. Could be just part of one."

"Like somebody got cut up—in pieces?" Somehow that option felt even worse.

"It's a possibility."

"Frank. I want to get out of here."

"We can't just leave. This needs to be investigated."

"Oh please—."

"Don't worry. I'm not going to do this on my own. We need to get the sheriff out here and then we will need a forensic team."

"Okay, so can I—can we go?"

Frank stood, pulled his cell phone from his pocket and flipped it open. Then he shrugged. "No service out here. We need to go back to where I'm parked."

"Think you'll have service there?"

"Probably not, but I've got the radio in my Blazer."

"So we can go?" I sneaked a final glance at my creepy discovery—there were two fingers showing now. Frank spread his vest over the excavation spot.

"See if you can find a stone to put on one corner," he said.

I searched around until I finally found a stone—about the size of a baseball. He put it on one corner of the vest, added another stone and then took out his pocketknife, opened it and drove the blade through the cloth into the ground.

"Guess that will hold it for a few hours." He picked up the mushroom sacks and handed one to me. "Let's go."

Frank started walking and I followed him, struggling to keep up with his long paces and wondering how he knew which way to go. We'd been wandering in the woods for a couple of hours and I had paid no attention to anything like landmarks, thinking that one tree looked pretty much like another. But Frank seemed to be moving with confidence, so I followed him without question.

We covered ground a lot faster than we did on the way in. The next thing I knew we crossed a little creek where I had to balance on a fallen log. After that he said, "I remember this stump. We're almost there."

Minutes later, I spotted the chrome trim of his Blazer reflecting sunlight through the trees, and felt a huge sense of relief. I didn't like the idea of being lost in the woods anywhere, but the thought of a dead body in the vicinity made the situation even worse.

We reached the Blazer and Frank opened his cell phone again, but apparently got no signal because he folded it up again. He pulled out his keys and unlocked the door of his vehicle, then sat down in the driver's seat. About a minute later, I heard the unmistakable crackle of the police radio.

"This is Kolowsky," he said. I've got a ten-fifty-four. Can you locate the sheriff for me?"

The response from the radio was mainly static, so loud and irritating that I walked away and sat on a rock, which turned out to be warm from the sun. I wished that I had brought along a thermos of coffee. And maybe a book to read. But how could I have known that the day was going to take such an unexpected turn?

I reminded myself that having a detective as the man in my life meant that I had to be ready for the unexpected. If I considered our relationship from his point of view, I had to admit that my job as a reporter made the whole thing a bit of a liability for him too. Cops seem to have a built in distrust of the press, perhaps with good reason.

Despite my assurances to the contrary, Frank has told me he harbors a fear that something he reveals in our pillow talk might end up in the paper. I've tried to tell him that I don't even write about crime or police stuff. My assignments tend toward less than exciting issues like village elections, long winded council meetings and features about farm kids with giant pumpkins.

My reverie ended when Frank stood and yelled, "Come on, we've got to get going."

I hurried over and slid into the passenger seat. "Are we going back to town?"

"Nope. I talked to Benny and he's going to meet us at the Russel Creek Bar." Frank started the engine and we headed down the road which wasn't really a road at all, more of a trail. It was the kind of thing I had learned to call a two-track, and this one had bushes and trees leaning in from both sides. Clearly the road wasn't used very much. It was so overgrown that low hanging limbs sometimes reached down far enough to scratch the windshield.

"Can we get out of here this way?" I said.

"I think the road dead-ends at the river."

"Then what are we going to do?"

"I'll turn around as soon as I find a wide spot."

The road seemed to be growing even more narrow, so the chance of finding a wide spot seemed remote at best. But I knew from Frank's tone that he didn't need me to tell him anything so obvious.

Eventually Frank found a clearing he deemed wide enough to accommodate a U turn. He muttered to himself as he stopped, backed up, twisted the wheel, jerked forward and then repeated the entire maneuver. Again. And yet again. Finally we were turned around and heading back down the road.

"If it was me, I would never be able to find this spot again," I said when we approached the spot where he had been parked.

"Why not?"

"There's no road signs and everything out here looks the same."

He put on the brakes and jerked to a stop. "You might be right—for once. It would make sense to leave some kind of marker."

"Marker—like what?"

"Something to serve as a flag."

"Like a strip of cloth?"

"Like a piece of clothing," he said. "I already left my vest in the woods. How about you take off your bra?"

"My bra? You've got to be kidding."

"No, I'm not. I saw it once in a movie—Crocodile Dundee, I think."

"You're not getting my bra. If you want underwear, use your shorts."

"Wrong shape. We need something to tie around a tree."

"Well, I'm not taking off my bra. I don't want Sheriff Benny to see my underwear—even if I'm not wearing it."

"Wait a minute. I think last summer you left a bathing suit in here."

"I knew it went missing. Why didn't you tell me you had it?"

Frank hopped out, opened a back door and started rummaging through the tools and camping gear and junk that always fill his back seat.

"Found it," he said as he pulled out the faded top of my old two-piece. "Just what I need."

"Did I give you permission to use it?"

He came around to my side and gave me the smile that always melts my resistance. "I already left my vest. It seems the least you can do."

"Oh, go ahead," I said at last. "It's just an old bathing suit."

"Thanks." He walked away and I watched as he selected a tree trunk and stretched the top around it. He couldn't seem to manage the fastening so he wound up tying the ends into a knot.

As he slid into the driver's seat beside me, he said, "You've already got a new suit, haven't you?"

"Sure, I've got another. But I cringe to think what Benny will say when he sees how you've used my old one."

"Don't worry. I won't even tell him it's yours."

"Benny will know," I said as he revved the engine and we were on our way again. "But please—no crass remarks about my bust size."

"What do you think we are—junior high kids?"

"On some level, yes. I think all men are."

"Okay, I promise. There will be no crass comments about your— bathing suit."

"Fine," I said, not exactly believing him. But then I had another thought. "I was just wondering—."

"Wondering what?"

"Do I have to come back here with you and the sheriff ?"

"You mean you don't want to help us dig up the body?"

"I'd rather not."

"Come on Tracy, where's your sense of adventure?"

CHAPTER THREE

"Maybe I don't have a sense of adventure," I said. "Or, let's say, finding those bony fingers was enough adventure to last me a lifetime."

"But we might need you."

"I don't see what for." I heard my voice take on a strident note.

"Hey, I'm just kidding. You don't need to be there."

"Great."

"I'm sure Sheriff Benny would prefer not to have you around. You being a member of the press and all."

"Well, good," I said with a sigh of relief. "So when we meet up with Benny, can you—maybe go with him—and let me drive home?"

"Can you drive this? The clutch is tricky."

"Of course I can. I drove it the night of your cousin's wedding when you were—when you had over indulged."

"Oh yeah, forgot about that. Sure. You can drive back to town. When we're done I'll have Benny bring me to your house." We emerged from the woods onto a gravel road, which was a relief after the bone jarring bounce of the two-track.

"So how much farther is it?"

"About two miles—we should pass the old Mobil station pretty soon and turn onto Scottville Road. The bar is on the next corner."

"How come you know these back roads so well? You've only been around a couple of years."

"Yes, but I've been hunting up here every fall for twenty years."

"Deer hunting?"

"Mostly. But the other reason I know this area is from responding to calls."

"Calls to 911?"

"Yes. Especially in November."

"Who makes these calls—the bears?"

"No, the management at the bar calls us. Sometimes they have fights."

"The bar? You mean the one where we're meeting Benny?"

"Yep, the Russel Creek Bar. Food's pretty good. I'm hoping I'll have time to get something to eat."

"Oh, great. I'm not sure I want to join you."

"Aren't you hungry? Breakfast was a long time ago."

This was true. But after our discovery in the woods, I was feeling a bit queasy. And Frank didn't make the bar sound very inviting. He hung a right at a corner marked by an abandoned gas station and we were finally on a paved road. I didn't see any more landmarks until we passed a rustic sign offering fresh brown eggs, with an arrow that pointed to a distant farm house with a big, red weather beaten barn.

Minutes later, Frank hit the brakes and said, "Here we are."

We slowed and pulled into the parking lot of the Russel Creek Bar, which turned out to be a single story building with an uninviting facade. There were no windows and the siding was a strange color which might have been green before the paint started peeling off. I looked around and saw at least a dozen pick-up trucks in varying states of disrepair.

"I don't understand how this place gets so much business," I said.

"Sunday is their biggest day."

"Why is that?"

"Guess the bars in Walkerville are closed on Sunday."

"Looks like we got here before Benny," I said, noting the absence of the sheriff's cruiser in the lot.

"Figured we would. And I seriously need a hamburger before I head back into the woods." Frank climbed out of the SUV while I sat still and eyed the building, trying to imagine what surprises might be waiting inside. "Are you coming?"

"Just give me a minute." I tried to maneuver his rear view mirror to give myself a peek at my reflection. I had been in plenty of bars in my lifetime but never anything quite like this one.

He came around and opened my door. "Hey, it's just a bar."

I gathered my courage and slid out of the seat. "You sure take me to nice places," I said. "Do you think I should have dressed up?"

"You look just right."

I reminded myself that I was a woman of the world as we walked across the dusty parking lot and made our way inside. Anyone who had frequented the Rathskeller Bar in Chicago ought to be able to handle this Podunk. The place we had entered was noisy, smoky and dark, with neon signs behind the bar advertising various brands of beer. We stood for a minute while Frank cased the joint and I waited for my eyes to adjust.

Near as I could tell, the customers were all men. Irrationally I was glad I hadn't surrendered my bra, although it's doubtful anyone would have noticed, since only a few of the denizens bothered to glance in our direction before they returned their attention to the television set.

Behind the bar was a woman who looked to be about fifty, with crew-cut orange hair and a brown kerchief tied around her neck.

"Hi Darlene," Frank greeted her as he took my arm and guided me into the room.

"Hey Frank," she replied. "How ya been?"

"Fine," he said as he led me to a Formica table with mismatched chairs. "Can you get your cook to rustle me up a hamburger. Or maybe two." He glanced at me. "Hamburger okay with you?"

"Sure," I said, figuring I could always give it to Frank if I couldn't eat it. There wasn't much that interfered with his appetite.

"This okay?" We sat down facing each other. My chair had a seat with a rip in the plastic cover.

"This is fine," I said, noticing that Frank's position gave him a good view of the entrance.

Darlene came to our table and said, "Want a beer?" Her faded green tee shirt had a picture of a tractor and said something about supporting farmers.

"Sure," said Frank, "a Millers. And Darlene, this is my friend Tracy."

Darlene smiled at me, her eyes wrinkling. "Hi Tracy, how ya doin'?"

"Pretty good." In a moment of female solidarity I said, "How do you like your job?"

"It's okay," she said with a wink. "Except for the customers. You want a beer?"

"Umm, got Miller Lite?"

"We do." Minutes later Darlene delivered our drinks and said, "Food shouldn't take too long."

"Had to wake him up, did you?"

"Something like that."

I took a drink and let my gaze move around the room. Because so many of the lot were wearing camouflage, the place had a quasi-military look. Some of the guys had beards and a couple of the younger ones sported tattoos. Eventually my attention settled on a man sitting alone who wore a red bandanna on his head and kept fingering his scruffy gray beard. He wasn't watching the ball game and he seemed to be talking to someone who wasn't there.

I was going to ask Frank about the guy when Darlene came over with our burgers. I took a bite and decided that maybe I was hungry after all. A few minutes later, the place went quiet. Because I had my back to the door, it took me a moment to understand the reason for the silence.

I turned around and saw Sheriff Benny Dupree walking toward us.

Everybody knew this man. Benny Dupree had been the elected sheriff of Cedar County for going on twenty years. He was tall, broad shouldered and bald, with only the shiny pate to suggest that he was pushing sixty and pushing it pretty hard. Dupree was in uniform, with the official insignia on his sleeve, the silver badge on his chest and a belt full of gadgets that included a holstered pistol.

"Hey there, you two," Benny said as he approached.

Frank stood and said, "Glad you could make it. We're almost done here. Want anything?"

"No, just had lunch."

He waved away Darlene who had started to come out from behind the bar. Benny took a seat beside Frank and gave me a look that made me wonder if I had mustard on my face. I got the feeling that the sheriff wasn't very happy to find me there.

Benny knew who I was. One of my first work assignments had been to interview him after a particularly close election and, after that, there was that body I found on the beach. Benny generally made an effort to tolerate me because good ink is always important to an elected official. But, after I started dating Frank, he seemed to consider me a bit of a liability.

The noise level at the bar slowly returned to normal.

Benny leaned over and spoke to Frank in a stage whisper. "So you two found yourself a body?"

"Something like that," said Frank. "I'll tell you about it when we get outside."

CHAPTER FOUR

Frank, the sheriff and I walked out of the Russel Creek Bar and paused in the parking lot. The two men stood together near the sheriff's car and I stayed over by Frank's SUV to give them the illusion of privacy. It was only an illusion, however. I was still close enough to hear every word they said.

"Looks like we found a body out in the woods," said Frank.

"Looks like?" said Benny.

"In a shallow grave," Frank said, looking around to see if anyone else was within earshot. "All we saw was a hand sticking out of the ground. Actually, it was Tracy who found it—she sort of sat on it."

Benny glanced at me with a humorless smile. "Guess she's good for something." Then his smile vanished. "What we gonna do with her?"

"Send her back home in my Blazer," said Frank.

"Sounds like a plan," said the sheriff. "And tell her to keep her mouth shut."

"Guess you heard that," said Frank as he walked over and handed me the keys to his SUV. "Do you know how to get back to town?"

"Not really."

Frank gestured toward the road we had come in on. "Go out that way, take the first right. After a couple of miles, take a left. After that, stay on paved road and keep going west. When you hit Old 31, go north. Then turn off when you hit Arrowhead Drive."

"Okay, got it." I didn't feel nearly as sure as I sounded, but didn't want to look dumb in front of Benny.

"And don't forget the morels. When you get home, slice them open and soak them in salt water. I should be at your place before dark."

"Fine," I said as I unlocked his vehicle. "You two have a good afternoon." "See you back at the ranch," said Frank. He touched my arm briefly before he went to join the sheriff.

As soon as Benny and Frank had left in the sheriff's car, I fired up the Blazer and headed out. I knew I should have written down Frank's directions, but I couldn't locate any paper and I didn't want to hang around the bar after they had gone. I probably could have remembered more if I had not been distracted by the image of a bony hand that kept intruding on my thoughts.

I did my best to follow the directions, but soon found myself on a gravel road that curved left and took me in the wrong direction. I thought about turning back, but decided to keep going until I hit an intersection. The gas gauge was creeping toward empty. Finally I hit a crossroad. I looked at the sun and did my best to continue westward. After crossing a couple of bridges, I came to a paved road which turned out to be Old 31—and that led me to Arrowhead Drive. That's when I knew where I was and started to breathe more easily.

As I passed the sign that said, "You are entering Shagoni River," I marveled again at my decision to relocate from Chicago to a village so small that it hardly merits a dot on most road maps. It was almost two years now since I had come to town in the wake of my grandfather's death and managed to land a job at the village weekly.

In the course of those two years, I had learned some local history. The town owed its existence to a confluence of waterways—Shagoni River, Arrowhead Lake and the big lake to the west, Lake Michigan. Early lumbermen had floated trees downriver to Arrowhead Lake, where the logs were loaded onto schooners and delivered to port cities around the Great Lakes.

Now, of course, everything had changed.

The lumber industry was gone and Shagoni River was a beach town, deathly quiet during the winter but a mecca for beach goers and fishermen in the summer. This meant that spring was the favorite season for most of us—with good weather but not too many tourists.

I felt a swell of pride when I spotted my very own house. Set on a gentle hill, it was surrounded by tall oaks, spreading maples, and lilac bushes that were just beginning to show a touch of lavender. My grandfather had left it to me when he died.

The century-old inheritance proved to be both a blessing and a curse. The place was large—two stories plus an attic, with a wraparound porch and a squeaky swing. I had never owned a house before, so I was ill prepared to deal with the problems that kept arising, each more expensive than the last. But with the help of friends and neighbors, I had managed to keep the heat on, the roof patched and the water running.

I pulled into the driveway and spotted my neighbors, Les and Daisy Tattersall, who were in their yard. I parked and went over to say hello to the pair whose recent wedding had been the primo social event of the winter. Les, who had just passed his eightieth birthday, was wielding a shovel while Daisy, not much younger, was on her knees in the dirt.

"Whatever are you two doing?" I said by way of a greeting.

Les appeared grateful for the interruption. "She says we have to get these durn things planted." He straightened up and leaned on his shovel. "I'm not sure why."

Daisy shook her head as though she couldn't believe her husband's ignorance. "Because they're dahlias. You know about dahlias don't you, Tracy?"

"Nothing," I said with a shrug. "Except, of course, they're beautiful."

Daisy held out a pair of brown bulbs for my inspection. "Well, you dig them up in the fall and plant them again in the spring. I've done it for years. I told Les when I married him that I wouldn't give up my dahlias. I brought them with me."

"I think she married me so she'd have help digging." Les groaned and bent over with a hand pressed to his back. "I tell you Tracy, this woman is killing me."

"Maybe she is, Lester, but I suspect that you are enjoying it."

The twinkle in his eye made me think I was right. "So where is Frank?" he said as he took in the presence of the Blazer parked behind my Honda.

"Oh, he's—ah—he's not with me." I stalled while I searched for a sufficiently vague answer. I remembered stern warnings from both Frank and the sheriff that I was not to say anything—to anyone— about our ghoulish discovery in the woods. "I mean, I drove home alone. He was detained on—on some business."

Now both of them peered at me in undisguised curiosity. "Weren't you two going for morels today?" said Daisy.

Darn! Why did the woman have such a great memory? I considered offering a lie, decided she would sniff it out in a minute. "Yes, we went for morels. And we found some too."

They both nodded, their bespectacled eyes on me as they waited for more information.

I took a deep breath, just to gain time. "The—ah—Sheriff Dupree will be bringing Frank home in a little while." That was really more than I wanted to share, but they were bound to see the sheriff's car when it arrived. I decided that the best move now would be a hasty exit. "Okay, I'll let you two get back to your work. Didn't mean to interrupt."

And with that I fled back to my own property, before they could fire any more questions at me. Then I feared I was being rude so I turned around and said, "If Frank and the sheriff find anything important, you'll read about it in Wednesday's paper."

They both waved and fell into a conversation that I couldn't hear. Maybe they thought I was protecting the secret location of Frank's morel patch. Such secrecy was not uncommon among local mushroom hunters. On the other hand, that didn't explain the presence on the scene of Sheriff Benny Dupree.

In any case, I had done my best.

I retrieved the mushrooms and carried them inside, with a stop on the way in to empty my mailbox. I put the morels in the kitchen and took a look at the mail. There was a colorful postcard in the mix but the telephone rang before I had time to examine it. I dropped the mail on my desk and went to answer the phone. It was my friend Jewell.

"Hi Tracy," she said. "I'm glad you're home. I really need to talk. Is this a good time?"

"I always have time for you," I said. "And let me guess. Are you maybe fretting over Sarah's baby shower?"

Jewell's only daughter Sarah was completing her last semester at the University of Michigan. And that's not all she was completing. Sarah was also in the third trimester of pregnancy.

"You are so perceptive," Jewell said with a laugh. "I thought I had all the time in the world to get ready. Now, suddenly, the shower is less than a week away."

"So what do we need to do before next Saturday?"

"I'm not even sure." She let out an exasperated sigh that I could hear over the phone. "When we talked to the manager at the Pomeroy Inn, she made it sound really simple—like they would take care of everything—food, drinks, decorations, greeting and seating."

"For the price they're charging, they should."

"I know. But all of a sudden, it's not so simple. I told them twenty guests but Sarah's bringing friends that will make it closer to thirty. So now they don't have enough chairs. Plus we need another punch bowl."

"Well, I'm pretty sure I've got one somewhere. And I can ask Lester where he and Daisy got those nice folding chairs for their reception."

"Thanks, that's a relief. I don't know why I'm stressing so much over this."

"Maybe it's because Mark and Sarah aren't married. And our generation is old fashioned enough to think it matters."

"You're probably right."

"So how is Paul handling this?" At Thanksgiving, Jewell's husband had been aghast and nearly hostile when Sarah and her boyfriend Mark announced *their* pregnancy, as they called it.

"Paul won't even talk about it. Except to tell me I shouldn't be doing this shower."

"Why not, for heavens sake?"

"He said my giving her a baby shower means that I'm approving their unmarried status. Well I don't really approve—but this is my only daughter and—oh, I don't know, Tracy, I guess it's just a woman thing."

"I think you're right. We all love Sarah and we're excited about the baby. So just ignore Paul and enjoy becoming a grandmother. It's not something that happens every day."

"Thanks for the pep talk. I'm feeling better already. But enough about me—how was your weekend?"

"It was nice. Frank and I had dinner last night in Stanton and took in a movie. Today he took me out to look for morels."

"Did you find any?"

"Yes, but Frank found most of them. I tell you, those things are hard to spot. Then as we were going—." I stopped short, again reminding myself that I couldn't talk about the dead body—not even to my best friend.

So I did a quick segue and asked Jewell about her work life. She had recently become director of nursing at Cedar County Hospital in Stanton. Jewell said that two nurses had resigned and she was having trouble filling their positions.

"Nobody wants to go into nursing these days," she said. "I guess it's not glamorous enough."

"I think it's because women have so many other choices."

"You're right about that. I couldn't get Sarah to go anywhere near a hospital. So how are things at the newspaper?"

"Same old, same old." Now it was my turn to complain. "When I started the job, Marge promised me a raise after the first year, but then she conveniently forgot about it. Last week I dared to raise the question and she gave me a sob story about financial difficulties. By the time she was finished, I felt lucky to have a job."

"Maybe she's right. Maybe we both are."

Jewell and I talked for another ten minutes and, by the time we finished, the problems of our respective worlds felt manageable. That's the joy of having a best friend.

CHAPTER FIVE

The sheriff's car stopped in front of my house and Frank got out. When I met him on the front porch, his first question was about the mushrooms. "Did you remember to soak the morels?"

"Yes, of course. They're on the kitchen counter. I made a salad and I've got some leftover lasagna to warm up."

"Sounds great."

Frank went straight to the kitchen, washed his hands and proceeded to drain the morels.

"So what did you and the sheriff find out there?"

"I'll tell you later." Sometimes Frank is a man of few words and this appeared to be one of them. Cooking the morels was clearly more important to him than talking about a dead body. I helped him pat the mushrooms dry and watched as he rolled them in flour and seasoning. We located my cast iron skillet and he asked me for butter.

I tried to hand him a bottle of olive oil but he looked at the bottle like it was some kind of poison. "Don't you have any butter?"

"Well, yes but—."

"They have to be cooked in butter. Believe me, I know. I tried olive oil once and it was a disaster."

"Sure, okay." I opened the refrigerator and handed him a stick of butter. "Why did you try the olive oil?"

"I was on a health kick and trying to lose weight."

My boyfriend Frank is about six two and weighs well over two hundred pounds. I like the fact that he is a big guy. I'm pretty tall myself and it feels good to be with someone who doesn't make me feel like an Amazon. As for his weight—he's probably a little over the insurance company standards, but he looks good to me. As for the twice broken nose—I think it gives him character.

Frank melted the butter, then slowly added the mushrooms, which sputtered and hissed in the hot butter. While he did that, I microwaved the lasagna and set the table. As soon as the morels were done, he put them on a platter and brought them to the table. The wrinkled brown fungus had been transformed into crispy critters that were hardly recognizable but smelled heavenly.

I cautiously took a first bite and pronounced them edible. On the second bite I decided they were delicious. "Now I understand why people go traipsing through the woods for these things," I said.

"It's the only way to get them. Plus it's a good reason to get outdoors in the spring."

"Amazing that there is one bit of nature we haven't been able to domesticate." We ate in silence for a few minutes and then I couldn't wait any longer. "You and Benny were gone quite a while. What happened out there?"

He waited a beat before he answered. "I hate to admit it—but it took us quite a while just to find the place."

"You got lost?"

"Let's say a little bewildered."

"Was this before or after my bathing suit top?"

"Both. First we drove past it. Then we came back and parked, but still wandered around longer than we should have before we found my vest and the two rocks. Guess I should have tied something around a tree out there."

"At least you found it. Then what?"

"We dug around—cautiously."

"Did you use shovels?"

"No—just our hands. It was a matter of not destroying evidence."

"I guess that makes sense."

"We got far enough to figure out that it's likely an entire body. We took some photos—but Benny and I both knew we should get some forensics people out there before we do any more digging."

"What have you seen so far?"

"The rest of the hand—and then we found the skull. It looked to be—." He stopped, studying his plate as though it held some secret.

"Looked to be what?"

Frank looked up at me. "Judging by the size of the hand and the skull, we think it was—a woman."

Suddenly the bony hand in the woods had become a person—and a woman at that. Somehow this information made it feel more personal. I tried to imagine her last moments. *Who had put her there and why?*

But I couldn't draw Frank into any speculation. He ignored my questions, making it clear that he didn't want to talk about the body any more. After supper we cleared the table and then sat in the porch swing, watching the sun slide down the western sky.

"Thanks for taking me out in the woods."

"Thanks for coming. It wouldn't be spring without morels."

"Of course, there was that—what you might call a surprise ending—."

"Have you talked with anyone—about that?"

"I tried not to. Les and Daisy saw me come in and I went over to say hello. They were curious about why I was driving your Blazer and you weren't with me. I told them as little as I could without being downright rude. No doubt they were watching when the sheriff brought you home."

"How much do they know?"

"They know that you and I were going to look for mushrooms. I told them that you'd been detained on business—and that's why I came back alone."

"I know some of the guys at the bar were pretty curious. I just hope we don't have any surprise visitors out there tomorrow."

"I think the place would be pretty hard to locate. I mean, even you had trouble finding it again."

"Let's hope you're right." Frank put an arm around my shoulders and I leaned against him. The porch swing squeaked as we sat and watched the barn swallows dive down from trees in search of insects for their supper. "Guess we both have to work tomorrow," he said, stifling a yawn.

"Unfortunately. Monday always comes."

It was close to ten o'clock when Frank left. I thought about turning on the television but decided in favor of a hot bath and a good night's sleep. But then, when I got into bed, my brain didn't want to shut down. The events of the afternoon kept running through my mind like a bad movie.

When sleep did come, it was restless—with dreams about a bony hand reaching out and a woman screaming. I felt as though I had just dropped off when the alarm clock rang, signaling the start of my work week.

I got myself to the office by eight, in an effort to avoid yet another lecture on punctuality from Marge Enright, my boss at the Shagoni River News. Marge used to lecture me a lot about punctuality and myriad other subjects, but one of her favorites was my appearance. This always struck me as ironic since Marge, to put it kindly, was badly dressed with a ridiculous beehive hairdo leftover from the sixties.

I said good morning to Norma, our receptionist, and headed for my desk in a corner of the general purpose space we call the newsroom. Only two people at the paper have an actual office and I am not one of them. I grabbed a cup of coffee, turned on my computer and was well into a story about the township cemetery when Norma came in.

"Marge wants to see you in her office."

"Right now?"

"I'm pretty sure."

I grumbled and finished my sentence, then saved the document before I walked down the hall to the editor's office. The door was open so I walked in and found Marge at her desk, staring at the computer screen. She acknowledged me with a gesture which meant I was supposed to wait until she was free—so I slid into the plastic chair that we underlings refer to as the hot seat.

Minutes later, she turned her attention to me. Marge had recently lost some weight and, quite possibly, had gone clothes shopping. Her bright pink blouse had a bow at the collar and was matched by a pair of plastic earrings shaped like daisies. I'm sure she was proud of her new appearance but I was still having trouble adjusting to the change.

"So Tracy, how was your weekend?"

This unexpected burst of congeniality put me a little off balance. Normally Marge doesn't give a fig about anybody's personal life, as long as we show up on time and able to function.

"It was fine," I said. "Did some yard work—didn't go anywhere special." I really didn't want to share any details of my private life.

But Marge just sat there looking at me while she tapped a pencil on her desk. "Weren't you with Benny and Frank out at the Russel Creek Bar yesterday?"

Sometimes I wonder if Marge has me under surveillance. "Well, yes," I said cautiously. "You may have heard about something happening out there in the woods."

"Yes, I did hear something."

I felt like I was backed into a corner. "I believe that Sheriff Dupree is planning to be out there today."

She nodded. "Jake and I talked early this morning. Jake is planning to stop by the sheriff's office before he comes in." At this point she looked past me into the hallway. "So look who's here."

I turned and saw the bulky figure of Jake Billington approaching. Generally I can recognize Jake by his smell alone—a heady mixture of cigar smoke, sweat and Old Spice. I am always happy to see Jake. Of all the people at the newspaper, he is the person I feel most comfortable with, despite his gruff demeanor. Since I never knew my father, it's possible that Jake fulfills some need for a paternal figure.

"Morning, Jake," said Marge. "Did you catch up with the sheriff?"

"Benny was gone," Jake said, with a shake of his head. "Nobody would tell me where he is, or when he might be back. Acted like it was some kind of top secret."

"I think Tracy probably knows something about that," said Marge.

I paused for a moment, considering my options. Frank had cautioned me not to tell anyone what we found in the woods—so once again I felt like I was between a rock and a hard place.

But I knew that my information would be more accurate than anything that might be churning through the gossip mill by now. And I was pretty sure that the sheriff would be obliged to make some kind of public statement before the day was over.

"Okay," I said at last. "Frank and I were out in the woods yesterday looking for mushrooms. We stumbled across something—it looked like a hand sticking out of the dirt."

"A human hand?" said Marge.

"That's what it looked like. And today Frank and the sheriff were heading out there with a forensic team to—well, you know, dig around some more."

Marge looked triumphant as she threw down her pencil. "This will definitely go on the front page. We'd better clear some space for it."

"We can hold that feature about the exchange students," I said.

"Right. And move the Farm Bureau piece to page three. Jake, how much space do you think you'll need for this new story?"

"How in blazes would I know? It could be half a page—or it could be one paragraph if I can't find anyone to tell me anything." At this point, Jake moved closer to me and said, "Do you think you could tell me how to get out there?"

Uh oh. No wonder Frank had cautioned me against talking. In a flash I realized that we were moving uncomfortably close to the very situation Frank wanted to avoid—reporters with cameras and tape recorder stalking him while he tried to work. How could I avoid letting Frank down? All of this ran through my mind while Jake stared at me, waiting for an answer to his question.

"Well," he said, "could you?"

"Sorry, what did you ask me?"

"Could you tell me how to get out there? To the place in the woods."

"Oh, the place—in the woods?" I wondered if I was sounding like an idiot. "I'm sorry, Jake, but I don't think I could get you anywhere close. I didn't pay any attention going in and then, on the way home, I got lost." This was mostly true.

"Were you out by the Russel Creek Bar?"

"Well, yes. We did stop there."

"Did you notice an old gas station—one that's been closed for a while?"

"Um, I don't think so. I don't remember any." That was one lie, maybe two. "Sorry. The whole thing had me pretty shook up." I shrugged, indicating that I just wasn't able to remember anything else.

Jake shook his head, suggesting that he didn't believe me. "I'll keep trying the sheriff on his cell," he said. "If he doesn't answer, I'll go over to Stanton this afternoon. If I don't get anything today, I'll haunt them tomorrow until I get a statement."

Stanton is the county seat and our weekly paper goes to press at the end of the work day on Tuesday.

"Let's finish all the stories we have started," said Marge, "and re-arrange page one. We're bound to have something by tomorrow and we'll leave space for it."

That seemed to settle the matter for the time being. I returned to my desk while Jake went out to cover a meeting. I had two stories to write and three more to complete, all of them requiring phone calls to officials who were in no hurry to reply to my increasingly frantic messages.

But I kept my cool and the rest of the day went by without any further crisis. I didn't see Jake again and that was a relief. By the time I left at the end of the day, no one had asked me anything else about the body in the woods.

When I got home, my message light was blinking. I pushed the button and was pleased to hear Frank's voice saying, "Call me as soon as you get home."

So I called and he answered. "Hi Frank," I said. "It's good to hear from—"

He cut me off. "I want to know what you told Jake."

"What do you mean, what did I tell Jake?"

"What I mean is the SOB found us. He was out in the forest, parked on the access road, but only because we had found a gate we could lock. When we came out, he was waiting."

My throat went dry. "Oh, Frank—honestly, I don't know how—."

"I was in the car with the sheriff and, when I got out to open the gate, your buddy Jake started peppering me with questions. I really wanted to punch him in the nose."

"You didn't, did you? Hit him, I mean."

"No. All I said was 'no comment' and asked him to step aside. Which he did. But he got a photo of the meat wagon when it came out."

"Frank I am so sorry that happened, but I don't think it was anything I said."

"It had to be you, Tracy."

"Listen to me," I said, feeling my neck getting hot. "I swear I did not tell Jake where you guys were going."

"You must have said something."

"Look—when I got to work this morning, both Marge and Jake had heard about a body in the woods. A lot of people saw us at the bar. They knew that you were not meeting up with Benny by accident. But I absolutely did not give away the location."

"I don't believe you."

"Are you calling me a liar? You've no right—."

"I've got to go."

"Frank, please listen—." I stopped talking when I realized there was no one on the other end of the call. The phone that was silent except for a dull hum.

CHAPTER SIX

I tried calling back but Frank didn't answer. After half an hour, I tried again and then an hour later with the same results—zilch—zero—nada. For a while I paced around the house, trying to figure out what I had done wrong, but I couldn't think of any way that I might have handled things differently—other than not going to work at all, which wasn't really an option. The bottom line was that Frank had his job and I had mine.

Eventually I made myself some supper, but didn't eat much. I was upset because Frank was angry and it seemed unfair of him to go all silent on me. I was angry at Jake for stalking the forensics team—but also, I was trying to figure out how Jake had found them. Did I reveal more than I thought I had? Was there some detail I had allowed to slip? I went over every word that I had said. And meanwhile, of course, I kept wondering if Frank would ever speak to me again.

I tried to call Jewell but nobody answered. I tried watching television, but found all of the programs unbearably stupid. I tried to read a book, but kept losing my place at the end of each line. Finally I tried calling Frank one last time, and when I heard his voice inviting me to leave a message, I said some bad words (but only to myself) before I gave up and went to bed.

It took me a long time to fall asleep and I'm not sure what time it was when I finally dropped off. But, the next thing I knew, a harsh ringing sound had jarred me awake. Reluctantly, I opened one eye and saw that it was still dark—so why was my alarm was ringing in the middle of the night? I reached out and punched the snooze button but the sound didn't stop—because the sound wasn't coming from the clock. My telephone was ringing.

Could it possibly be Frank? Was he so stricken with remorse that he was calling in the middle of the night to apologize? It seemed unlikely—but the ringing didn't stop. Whoever wanted me was serious about it. I rolled out of bed and stumbled into the living room to pick up.

It wasn't Frank. It was Marge.

"The Pomeroy Inn is on fire, and you are the only one in town. So get yourself over there."

"You mean now?"

"Of course, I mean now."

"But Marge, it's the middle of the night."

"Actually, it's five-thirty in the morning. Take your camera. Kyle should be there soon but photo ops don't wait. Especially when a landmark is burning down."

"Okay," I said as the fog of sleep began to lift. "I'm on it."

I had seen young people wearing pajamas in public and this seemed like the opportune moment to join that fashion trend. So I stayed in my pajamas, wiggled into a pair of shoes and threw on an old army jacket that Frank had given me. Fortunately the jacket was stocked with a pencil and note pad in one pocket, and my camera in the other.

The acrid smell of smoke hit me the moment I stepped out of my door. I got in my car, drove four blocks north, and that's when I saw the glow. Two blocks west and I saw flames. One more block was as close as I was going to get because of police barricades. There were cars parked all around, most of them police but some civilians—probably just gawkers. And now the press had arrived.

I parked and got out. The three story building had flames shooting out of nearly every window, undeterred by the streams of water pouring in. There were six fire trucks on the scene and another one making its way past the barricade. There were firefighters everywhere, more than I could count. All of the firefighters were focused on the building, except for a handful who were spraying the trees at the perimeter of the property.

I did my best not to get in anyone's way as I moved around the scene and took pictures from a variety of angles. Photography was definitely not my forte, but it came with the job. That done, I looked around for someone to talk with. I recognized Fred Meeker, a dentist who serves on the village council. Like me, he was in pajamas, but wearing a trench coat that covered most of the stripes.

Meeker was talking with two other men, who were dressed but disheveled. Tragedy eliminates social barriers, so I stepped up to the trio and said, "Anyone heard any theories on how this started?"

The dentist shook his head and said, "Might have been the wiring—the building is over eighty years old."

A short man with a goatee said, "You write for the paper, don't you?"

"Yes, but I'm not going to quote you."

"That's good," he said. "Because—off the record—there's been some talk about arson. It's just talk, you understand."

"Arson," I said. "But who—or why?"

"Maybe the owner," said the other guy, who was wearing his baseball cap backward. "I heard that Clint Pomeroy had this place mortgaged to the hilt—and he was having some trouble making payments."

This was news to me. Everything I had heard about the Pomeroys indicated that they were one of the most well off families in town. I wanted to ask the guy where he got his information, but just then I saw a dark haired young man approaching. I left off and trotted over to the newcomer.

Kyle Nelson is our youngest reporter and also the official photographer. His shaggy black hair was uncombed but he was fully dressed and had a camera hanging around his neck. He saw me and stopped.

"How long you been here?" he said.

"Just a few minutes."

"Heard anything?"

"All speculation." I shoved my camera into my coat pocket. "You go ahead with photos. I'll try to get some statements."

Kyle nodded agreement and moved on.

I looked around for someone in authority and spotted Fire Chief Jackson talking with two of his crew. All three of them were in that black gear with yellow stripes that reminds me of a bumble bee. I waited until the chief was finished talking with his crew before I approached.

"I'm Tracy Quinn," I said, "with the Shagoni River News."

Of course Jackson had seen me before—but in my pajamas and bed head, who knew? Plus it's important to let officials know when they are on the record.

"Can't tell you much," said Jackson. "A neighbor noticed the fire and called it in around four-thirty. Looks like the fire started in the back of the building."

"Any idea what may have been the cause?"

He shook his head and said, "We have professional investigators for that. " Then he left to go meet a fire truck from Stanton that had just been waved through the barricades.

I wandered through the circle of bystanders to see if I could locate Clint Pomeroy, the owner of the building, but he was nowhere to be found. I managed to find the neighbor who had called in the fire. Jeff Nusbaum, a retiree, said he had gotten up to use the bathroom when he smelled the smoke, saw the fire and called 911.

"I hope it doesn't get any of our trees," he said.

"I guess we're all lucky you woke up when you did," I said.

"Oh yeah. Nothing like the aging prostate."

I spoke to several more onlookers and the chief of police but none of them offered any new information. After nearly an hour of breathing smoke, I was developing a cough, so I decided it was time for me to go. I found Kyle and told him I was leaving and would see him back at work. Then I went home where I showered, got dressed and drank some coffee before heading to the office.

I arrived at seven-thirty and found most of the staff already there, fueled with coffee and doughnuts. Marge called an impromptu meeting and, when we were assembled, gave us all new directions.

"The front page, obviously, needs to be rearranged again. And the headline story now is the fire at the Pomeroy Inn."

"Is it a total loss?" said Jake, who had just walked in.

"Looks that way to me," said Larry, our graphics guy, who had done a drive-by on his way in.

"That place has been around forever," said Marge. "We need to do some history on it."

So Marge parceled out the tasks. Jake was still working on the story about the body—but it was no longer the headline piece. Kyle and I were assigned to write the primary fire story. After that, I was supposed get a statement from Clint Pomeroy and Kyle was to work with the graphics department on photos. It was late morning when Kyle and I submitted our story for Marge's approval.

Then I tried to call Clint Pomeroy. Marge said he had a business in Grand Rapids and lately had been spending most of his time there. So I tried the number listed in the phone directory and another one that Marge had on her rolodex. I got no answer at either one which wasn't a big surprise. He probably had a cell phone.

I decided to revisit the fire scene, thinking Pomeroy might be there.

When I arrived at noon, it was clear that the building was gutted. The barricades were still up, three trucks were still on the scene and people were hosing down the ruins. A brisk wind had come in off the lake and was stirring up smoke and ashes. The crowd of onlookers was bigger than ever.

I spotted Tom Lemar, the State Farm insurance agent, who was taking his own photos and making notes on a clipboard. I asked him if he had seen Clint Pomeroy.

"You just missed him," said Lemar. "Pomeroy drove up from Grand Rapids when he got the news. He was here for about an hour, but now he's gone again."

I asked Lemar if he had a cell phone number for Pomeroy.

"I, do but I, ah, guess I really shouldn't give it out."

"Sure, I understand."

Frustrated, I went back to the office where I found some of the staff in the break room. I told Marge I wasn't getting anywhere with finding Pomeroy.

"He's probably trying to avoid us," she said.

"Can't blame him," said Larry.

"Guess you're right," said Kyle. "I don't think anybody would be ready to face the press after seeing their family legacy go up in flames."

"So just put that on hold for now," Marge said. "Tracy, do some research and put together a piece on the history of the place. There should be plenty of stories in the archives."

"I was thinking about lunch—."

"Norma brought in sandwiches," she said. "We're all eating here."

So I grabbed a tuna sandwich and poured myself another cup of coffee. And that's when it hit me. This was more than a big news story—this event had a personal impact. Jewell was planning to hold Sarah's baby shower at the Pomeroy Inn on Saturday.

Clearly that wasn't going to happen.

I called Jewell at the hospital. It took a few minutes to get through to her. "Jewell, have you heard about the Pomeroy Inn?"

"What happened?" she said lightly. "Did somebody bomb the place?"

"No Jewell, no bomb. At least I don't think so—but the place caught fire early this morning and, well—it's gutted."

Silence.

"Jewell, are you there?"

"Yes, I am, I guess. But this means—."

"This means you won't be having Sarah's shower—not there anyway."

"But—everything was all set—it's only four days away."

"I know."

"What can we do?"

"Don't worry," I said, striving to sound a lot more confident than I felt. "We'll figure something out. We'll still have the shower."

"But Tracy—where??"

"I don't know—but we'll think of something. Sorry, Jewell I've got to go." I felt bad about cutting Jewell off, but I had to do it. Jake had just walked in and I suddenly remembered that I needed to talk to him—in private.

CHAPTER SEVEN

I followed Jake into his office and accosted him before he had a chance to sit down.

"I'm in deep doo doo," I said, "and it's all your fault."

"Me?? What did I do?" He looked at me with a wide eyed expression of innocence.

"Jake, you know exactly what I'm talking about. I want to know how you found the crew in the woods that was exhuming the body. Frank thinks I drew you a map or something."

"Oh, that." He tossed his briefcase on his desk and sat down. "You and I both know that's not what happened. You didn't give me any directions."

"You and I know that—but Frank doesn't. He's furious with me."

"I am sorry about that."

"He's furious because you found them." Jake motioned me to a chair but I remained standing. "You know cops don't like reporters hanging around."

"Tracy, I was just doing my job. The sheriff wasn't returning my calls. When we're on deadline, I can't wait around for these guys to issue their official statements."

"I still don't understand how you found them. Was it something I said?"

"Not really. I went out to the Russel Creek Tavern, drove past the old Mobil station and took the first road into the Manistee National Forest. Once in the woods, I just examined all the side roads for evidence of traffic. Most of them hadn't been used since fall. But then

I found one that showed tire tracks—in fact, a lot of tire tracks. So I turned down that road and just followed the trail, so to speak."

"Well, aren't you smart."

"But I stopped when I came to a turnoff that had a gate across it."

"And waited for them to come out."

"That's what I did."

"Okay then. Now I know how you did it. I just hope I can convince Frank that I wasn't a blabbermouth."

"If you want me to talk to Frank, I will. I didn't mean to cause any problems with your love life."

"Thanks, but no thanks." I didn't think my status with Frank would be improved by any further intervention from Jake.

"Okay then—I gotta write up this story."

I started to leave, then paused in the doorway. "Wait a minute. When you saw the sheriff, did he give you anything you could use?"

Jake shrugged. "Said a body had been exhumed. Said it appeared to be a woman. Said it had been in the ground all winter."

So now Jake knew exactly as much as I did. The story would be in tomorrow's paper and everyone in Cedar County would have the information. But at least it hadn't come from me.

It was after six when I finally got away from work. I headed straight to Jewell's house, which had become my second home over the past two years. Jewell and her husband Paul have a ranch style home nestled among the birch and cedar trees that ring Arrowhead Lake, making it an ideal place to sip wine and watch the sunset.

Jewell had just come in from a run. She met me at the door in a turquoise track suit that matched her eyes. With her halo of soft blonde hair, she did not look old enough to be almost a grandmother. Jewell greeted me with a hug and a warm smile but the lines around her eyes betrayed distress.

"I drove by the Pomeroy Inn," she said, "because I just had to see for myself. It's for sure we won't be having Sarah's shower there."

"You're right about that. I understand it was a total loss."

"I talked to Sarah about re-scheduling but that isn't an option. Her friends have school obligations, graduations, weddings. But anyway, come on inside."

I followed Jewell into the kitchen where her husband was loading the dishwasher. Paul had played football in college and still had a pretty solid build, although his wire rimmed glasses always made me think of a professor.

He stood to give me a hug. "How's Frank?"

"He's okay," I said. "Haven't seen him since Sunday." I had already decided not to bring my problems into the mix.

"I hope you can help Jewell. She seems to think the world is coming to an end—and I haven't been much help."

"It's a girl thing," I told him.

"Have you had supper?" Jewell said as she took my coat.

"No, I came straight from work—but don't worry about—."

"That's what you were supposed to do. I fixed a plate for you and I'll just stick it in the microwave."

Minutes later I was eating beef stroganoff that rivaled the stuff my grandmother used to make.

Paul excused himself, saying he would be in his office. "Since our living room is not habitable at the moment," he added with a rueful smile.

From where I sat at the dining table, I saw what he was talking about. The furniture in the next room was clustered in the center of the carpet and covered with sheets. A ladder straddled the sofa. Jewell handed me a glass of wine and rolled her eyes at Paul's retreating back.

"Paul keeps telling me to cancel the shower—but he doesn't understand. It's something I really need to do. Sarah's my only daughter and this is my first grandchild."

"We need an alternate location. How many people are you expecting?"

"Between twenty and thirty. As you see, there's no way I can do it here. We took down the old paneling in the living room and put up drywall. The plaster is finished but now it needs to dry and the painters won't be here until Monday. The timing couldn't be worse. If only I had known."

"How could you? Nobody imagined that the Pomeroy Inn would burn down."

"The place is an institution At least it was. Tracy, what am I going to do?"

Jewell's eyes glistened with unshed tears. I heard myself say, "I suppose we could have it at my place. " Then I groaned inwardly and wished I could take back the words.

"Would you?" Her face brightened. "I mean I hate to even ask. It's such an imposition."

On that point she was right—I lived alone and liked it. Frank was my only regular visitor and he never cared what my house looked like. But this was different. It meant opening my home to a crowd of women, many of them strangers. The thought made me painfully aware of all the dust bunnies and spider webs I tended to ignore, not to mention the yellowed fixtures in the bathroom and cracked linoleum in the kitchen. I tried to back pedal.

"My place is big enough, I guess, but it's only got one bathroom and, heaven knows, I haven't done any spring cleaning."

But it was too late to retract my offer. Jewell was just so happy. "I'll help you clean house," she said. "Better yet, I'll hire someone to come in and do it for you."

"That would help a lot—if we can find anybody." I struggled to wrap my mind around the details. "I can get some chairs from Les and Daisy. But what about the food and punch?"

"I can do all of that myself. It's really no big deal."

And so the plan was in place. We talked for another hour and, by the time I left, Jewell had thanked me a dozen times. I was less than enthusiastic, but kept reminding myself of all the things that Jewell had done for me. At least it gave me something to obsess about other than Frank being mad at me and that unidentified body.

"90 YEAR OLD LANDMARK BURNS" was the headline across the top of Wednesday's issue of the Shagoni River News, set in type two inches high. I grabbed the paper and took it to my desk. Kyle and

I had collaborated on the primary story about the fire and Marge had even used one of my photos. There was also a sidebar I had written, explaining that the building was constructed in the early nineteen hundreds to accommodate visitors who came by boat from Chicago.

Also on the front page, but relegated to the lower right quadrant, was a story titled, "Body Found in National Forest." It was continued on page three with a photo of the ambulance pulling out of the woods. The piece ended with a request for anyone who might have information about the identity of the woman to please contact the Cedar County Sheriff's Department.

Marge was out of the office, which was a real blessing since I now had two things distracting me—the impending shower was only three days away, and Frank still hadn't called. After lunch I walked down to city hall, with hopes of seeing the village manager.

"Is Jim available?" I said to the clerk, Mamie, a seemingly ageless woman whose hair was styled in a helmet of waves.

"He's out of town today," she replied. "But he told me to give you this." Mamie smiled and I groaned as she handed over a thick stack of papers secured with a rubber band.

Back in the office, I reviewed the documents and tried to make sense out of the mind numbing pages of tables and graphs and statistics. The crux of the matter was that the village water supply contained arsenic, which sounded rather scary, but it turned out that arsenic was a naturally occurring element in groundwater. By the time I had read through enough letters and charts to create a rough draft of the story, it was time to call it a day.

I spent my evening at home, mainly on the phone. Jewell and I were both trying to find someone to clean my house. But the women I reached had no interest in taking on another job, no matter how much we were willing to pay. Jewell called and said she'd had no luck either.

"Our problem is the time of year," she said. "It's spring and these women are busy cleaning rental cottages. But don't worry, we'll find somebody."

"I certainly hope so. Time is running short."

"Hey, I read about the body in the woods. Was Frank involved with that?"

"Yes, he was." I tried to figure out how much I wanted to tell her. "He and Benny were out there on Monday. Guess they don't know who she is."

"That's creepy," she said.

I was tempted to tell her just how creepy it had been for me, but quickly decided I had better not breathe another word, to anyone, about my day in the woods.

After that, I broke down and called Frank but got his voice mail telling me to leave a message. Damn! Was he screening his calls? The thought made me so angry that I hauled out the vacuum and tackled my living room carpet. After that I started to scour the bathroom, but quit when I realized that bathroom scrubbing is a chore best done in the daylight.

The next morning I went to Stanton to cover the county board meeting and, as usual, shared the press table with reporter Ivy Martin. Ivy writes for the Manistee Chronicle, a daily about forty miles to the north, so we tend to see each other every couple of weeks whether we need to or not.

As the meeting wound up, Ivy pushed back her long dark hair, leaned toward me and said, "How about joining me for lunch?"

"I'd love to, but Marge wants me back at the office. Lunch meeting."

"Oh you're always full of excuses. I don't even believe you."

She was right. The lunch meeting was a total lie—and I didn't like telling lies. But my friendship with Ivy had been strained ever since she'd indulged in an indiscretion with Jewell's husband. Since then Ivy had apologized profusely for her bad judgment, and sworn on her girl scout honor that it would never happen again. But the situation left me feeling torn, because I didn't want to continue a friendship with Ivy, who had caused so much pain to Jewell.

On the other hand, I couldn't avoid Ivy completely. Short of finding a different job, which was not exactly an option.

"Next time," I promised. With that, I scurried out and drove straight back to the office, where I found Marge at the front desk, talking on the phone.

As soon as she saw me, Marge said, "Have you located Clint Pomeroy yet?"

I cringed and tried to hide my surprise. I had pretty much forgotten that I was supposed to track down the owner of the Pomeroy Inn. "He's still not answering his phone," I said.

"We need a follow up piece on the Pomeroy Inn. Some human interest about him and his family—didn't his great-grandfather build the place?"

"I don't know. You've been here longer than me."

"So find him. And then talk to people who worked there. Almost everybody who grew up in town worked for a summer at the Pomeroy Inn. Sort of a rite of passage. But most of all, you need to talk to Pomeroy."

"I'm on it," I said and headed for my desk.

"Wait a minute. Was there anything from the county meeting?"

"Um, let's see." I flipped through my notes. "Board is considering a county wide junk ordinance."

"Do we need one?"

"Depends on who you ask. Most townships are opposed. But the county board says that township officials are lax and they tend to ignore the problem of junk cars leaking oil into the ground."

"Okay. Sounds like a story. But talk to some township officials— get both sides."

"Of course." I headed for the lunch room. On my way, I passed Jake's office and he motioned me in.

So I ducked into his office. "Thought you might like to know," he said. "The latest word about the body—in the woods. Or maybe Frank has already told you."

"No—I, ah, haven't seen Frank." Thanks to you, dummy.

"The coroner told the sheriff it looks as though the woman buried in the woods is—or rather was—an Indian."

CHAPTER EIGHT

I stared at Jake. "Did the coroner mean she was Indian as in—from India?"

"No, no. Indian as in cowboys and Indians."

"I think the term you're looking for is Native American."

"Yes, you're probably right. Benny's not exactly up on this current terminology. But in any case, it should be helpful with identification."

"I'm sure it will. This narrows the field considerably. To what—less than two percent of the population?"

"Something like that."

"Okay, thanks for keeping me in the loop. Anything else—?"

"Her age was somewhere between forty and sixty."

"That's a wide range. Anything on how she died?"

"The sheriff doesn't want to publish any cause of death—but I get the feeling she was strangled."

"What do you mean, you get the feeling?"

"Based on what they didn't find—no bullet holes, no caved-in skull."

"So she was murdered."

"Well yes, but we already knew that, didn't we?"

"Yes, I suppose we did."

After a sandwich in the lunch room, I tried to work, but my mind kept wandering back to what Jake had told me. So a woman had been killed—a Native American woman. Did I know any native people? Well, yes, a few. There were the two women I interviewed when I did a story about the ghost dinners held every fall at the Indian Catholic

Church. And there was the man who demonstrated basket weaving at the folk arts festival held at the fairgrounds in April.

But surely if someone had been missing since last fall, the fact would have been reported. So it looked like the murder victim was not from around here. If that was the case, how had she ended up buried in the Manistee National Forest?

And when was Frank going to get over his snit and call me?

And how was I going to get my house clean in time for Sarah's baby shower?

By this time, both Jewell and I had been getting phone calls from friends who wanted to know if the shower was canceled. Daisy Tattersal had called me at work and, since Marge had left the building, I decided to call her back.

I reached Daisy and told her the shower was going to be at my house. I asked if we could borrow some of their folding chairs.

"Of course," she said. "Lester and I can bring them over today. Is your house locked?"

"Um no. I only lock it at night."

"Then Lester and I will bring the chairs over and that will be one less thing for you to worry about."

"Thanks a lot," I said. "But you'd better put the chairs in the back room. I haven't had time to do any house cleaning. To be honest, I didn't want to do this, but Jewell was upset at the thought of canceling—so I took it on."

"That was sweet of you."

"I'm starting to regret it. We couldn't find anyone to come in and clean so Jewell and I will have to work some magic before Saturday."

"Don't you worry about a thing," said Daisy, which was more or less her mantra when anyone she knew had any kind of problem. "Everything will work out fine."

"I hope you're right," I said, unconvinced.

Then I finally got to work, still trying to track down the elusive Clint Pomeroy. I tried his home number in Allendale, but got the answering machine again. I tried his business number in Grand Rapids and actually got a live person who said she was his secretary.

The secretary sounded as though she were eating something as she told me that Mister Pomeroy wasn't in and she didn't expect him today. Figuring she was pretty bored, I made small talk for a few minutes, made up something about a family emergency, and finally got her to give me a cell phone number.

Feeling very clever, I called the number but got a recorded voice telling me that the number I had reached was out of service. I tried a second time but got the same result. So, was this a technical error—or were people playing games with me? The whole thing was making me a little crazy.

I had about an hour left at work so I decided to do a search of the archives for the Pomeroy Inn. Fortunately, the paper had run a feature a few years back when the place celebrated its eightieth birthday.

I learned that the place was built in 1912, as a beach side resort, with most of the visitors coming from around Chicago. It was advertised as an upscale destination where people could bring their families to relax, swim and play croquet. A special boat ran from Chicago twice a week during the summer.

When auto travel became feasible, the place added more rooms and, later on, in the fifties, the dining room was expanded and opened to the public. Over the years, the accommodations had been used for family reunions, weddings and, more recently, business retreats. Before Clint Pomeroy took over, it had been owned by his parents, Charles and Ella Pomeroy. The article mentioned the passing of Ella.

I found Jake at his desk and asked him when Charles Pomeroy had died.

"About two years ago," he said.

"What do you know about Clint Pomeroy? Why is he so hard to find?"

Jake leaned back in his chair. "First of all, you have to understand the situation," he said. "By the time old Charlie let go of the place, Clint had made another life for himself—with a real estate business and a pretty expensive home down in Grand Rapids."

"Is he married?"

"Married late and divorced early, I believe. No kids."

"Does he spend any time up here?"

"Clint has a cottage on Arrowhead Lake but, for him, it's just a vacation place. I don't think he was very eager to take on the family business."

"I understand he's still paying off the mortgage."

"I wouldn't doubt it. As a rule, Clint was always trying out some scheme that was supposed to make him rich overnight. Most of the schemes never worked."

"Do you think he would have torched it—for the insurance money?"

"If so, it was a very stupid move—because nowadays it's really hard to get away with arson. Insurance companies have developed strict policies. They send in their own fire inspectors and won't pay until they're satisfied that the fire was truly an accident. I've heard of some cases dragging on for years."

"Not a way to make a fast buck."

"Not at all. Things any better with you and Frank?"

"I'll let you know," I said with a shrug. I wasn't ready to discuss my personal life with Jake.

I got home shortly after six and, as soon as I stepped on the porch, I knew that something was amiss. Someone was inside my house. It wasn't Frank—because his vehicle was nowhere in sight. I scanned the street, looking for an unfamiliar car as I recalled the unannounced visit I had received from my ex-husband a few months before. Hopefully he wasn't about to surprise me again.

Cautiously I opened the frosted glass door. In the hallway my nostrils flared at the scent of lemon furniture polish—and then I heard voices. Seconds later, I discovered Daisy and Les. She was mopping the kitchen floor and he was on a step ladder taking down the dining room curtains. The fireplace was already cleaned, the old tile shining.

I was too dumbfounded to speak.

Daisy smiled when she saw me and put down her mop. She made absolutely no apology for invading my space. "Tracy dear," she said, "we've got everything under control. We're going to take those curtains home with us tonight. I'll get them washed, starched and ironed and we'll hang them up tomorrow. While I'm doing the curtains, Lester will come over and wash your windows."

"If that's okay with you," said Lester as he came down from the ladder, with a hint of apology in his manner. He seemed to understand that I might be a little taken aback by his wife's over-zealous invasion of my home.

"I guess it will have to be okay," I mumbled, while I struggled with a number of emotional responses. *Certainly it was a relief to have my house cleaned, but they might have at least given me some warning—*

"Once Daisy heard about your situation she was determined to help—and you know there's no stopping this woman once she gets an idea in her head."

I took a deep breath and decided that since there was no stopping Daisy, short of locking all of my doors, I might as well let go of my indignation.

I gave him a hug and said, "Lester, I knew when you married Daisy it would be interesting having her for a neighbor—but I never expected anything like this."

"Me neither." Lester and I traded a commiserating look and then we both started laughing.

I made a pot of peppermint tea and the three of us shared it in my kitchen, which was cleaner than it had been in years. Daisy had scrubbed all the countertops, the stove, the microwave and even the refrigerator.

"I'm sorry you had to deal with my place being such a mess," I said. "This is the first time I've ever owned a house. Sometimes I just get overwhelmed."

Daisy shushed me. "Don't apologize," she said. "I really love cleaning house—especially an old place like this."

"It's true," said Les. "She went over my house from top to bottom— and that was before she moved in."

"So what else do you need for Saturday?" she said. "What about refreshments?"

"Jewell's taking care of the food and we're going to have punch."

"Will there be coffee?"

"I don't think so."

"Oh, you must have coffee. Some people will be driving a long way—and they'll appreciate a pick me up. I'll bring over my big coffee maker and my collection of cups and saucers."

I remembered Daisy's cup collection from their wedding party. "But Daisy, those are so delicate. What if somebody breaks one?"

"Oh, not to worry. I've got more than I need anyway. "

"Okay," I said meekly, and that seemed to settle the matter of coffee. And, for the moment, the whole baby shower issue was taken care of. But Daisy wasn't through with me yet.

"I read in the paper about a body in the woods," she said. "So is *that* what Frank was doing on Sunday?"

"Yes, he was. But I wasn't supposed to tell anybody about it."

"Oh, I understand. But well—this is a real mystery isn't it? I mean the part where we don't even know who she is."

"Yes, it is a mystery."

"Now Daisy," said Les, "don't you start in on this detecting business."

Daisy ignored him. "Do they know anything else about her—about how she died?"

"I guess all I can say is that it wasn't an accident."

"So that means—."

"Come on, Daisy," said Les. "I believe your book club meeting is tonight."

Daisy looked at her watch. "Oh, all right. I guess we need to go."

After my visitors left, the first thing I did was call Jewell. "You won't believe this, but my neighbors came over to clean my house."

"Les and Daisy?"

"Right. I got home and found they had taken over the place. At first I felt a little invaded—but then I decided that if they wanted to scrub my house, there was no use fighting."

"What a wonderful surprise. Maybe we can pay them something."

"I can tell you right now that they'll refuse. Les never takes any money in the winter for snow blowing my driveway and shoveling the porch."

"Then I'll try to think of something I can give them. Maybe a special rose bush."

"Oh sure, then poor Les will have to plant it."

She laughed. "You're right. I'll have to think of something else. But tell me, what do you think about Les and Daisy? Is she going to wear that poor man out?"

"If so, I guess he'll die happy."

We talked a while longer. I told her that Daisy was providing coffee and we reviewed other details about the event, now only two days away. After I hung up I noticed that my message light was blinking.

I pushed the button and heard Frank's voice. "Tracy, call me when you can." Shouldn't there have been apology in there somewhere? I debated for a few minutes before I called him—and when I did, the call went to voice mail.

I decided not to leave any message. Now that Frank was coming around, it made perfect sense to let him dangle for a while.

CHAPTER NINE

Saturday dawned cloudy and by noon a persistent drizzle was falling. The weather, however, failed to damped the enthusiasm of Jewell, who arrived shortly after noon, followed by her husband who carried in several boxes of supplies before he was dispatched from the scene.

"Some people think it's okay to have men at a baby shower," she said, "but I'm not one of them. Today it's strictly us girls."

"Fine with me," I said, looking at the boxes. "Where do we start?"

"Let's see—decorations, I guess. I'll start on that while you take the food to the kitchen. The dip should go in the fridge—put the ice ring in the freezer—everything else is okay at room temperature. And—do you have a step ladder?"

I directed Jewell to the step ladder and put the food in the kitchen. When I returned to the living room, Jewell was on the ladder attaching pink streamers to my chandelier. Following her instructions, I carried the ends of the streamers to the outer reaches of the room and taped them to the tops of window or door casings. We had just run out of streamers when we heard noise on the porch, followed by a knock.

"Come on in," I yelled.

Les and Daisy entered with Les toting the coffee maker and card table. Daisy had a can of coffee and a box of cups and saucers.

"Just put those down," Daisy said to her husband. "Now, how about you set up the folding chairs—and after that you can leave." Daisy seemed to share Jewell's position about the presence of men at a baby shower.

"Fine with me," said Lester. He brought the folding chairs from the back room and set up about half of them. And then he was gone.

For the next hour, I let Jewell and Daisy take charge of my house and did whatever they told me. They put a lace cloth on the dining room table and covered the card tables with pink plastic spreads. Jewell gave me the job of mixing punch, which suited my skill level, since all I had to do was open bottles and dump them into the punch bowl.

Daisy joined me in the kitchen where she filled the coffee maker and set it to brewing. The smell was heavenly and made me wonder how I had ever imagined we could get by without caffeine.

"Guess that's it for now," said Jewell.

"And just in time. So excuse me for a minute." I ducked into my bedroom, combed my hair and changed into a blouse and clean slacks.

"I think the coffee's ready and we all deserve some," Daisy said when I emerged. She filled three cups for us.

We took our coffee into the living room and collapsed onto the sofa. Before long, we heard a car outside, followed by the sound of doors slamming and high spirited voices.

"That must be Sarah," said Jewell. She jumped up and ran to the front door.

Minutes later, she was hugging her daughter, a tall and very pregnant blonde wearing a bright red maternity dress. Sarah had always been a beauty, but now she absolutely glowed, with the pink cheeks of a happy mother-to-be. She had three college friends with her.

The flurry of introductions was still in progress when another contingent arrived, this one consisting of two aunts and three cousins. One of the cousins had brought her four-year-old daughter, a girl with shiny black hair who looked to be adopted, based on her Asian features.

After that, everything became a blur as more people arrived and I was introduced to a number of Stephanies and Melanies and one each of Madison, Miranda and Madeline. Brightly wrapped packages formed a pyramid on one of the card tables. There were lots of hugs, congratulations and catching up on news.

Since Jewell was involved with her extended family I was grateful for the presence of Daisy as co-hostess. She was in her glory as she quietly circulated, making sure that every guest had a place to sit and a drink of either punch or coffee. Jewell mentioned that she had been in labor with Sarah for twenty-four hours and, after that, almost everyone there had a story to tell about their pregnancy, labor and or delivery.

Eventually, Jewell announced that everybody was present and it was time for the games to begin. Sarah's cousin June, a short round-faced girl, led us through her selection of baby games. Oh boy. How did I ever forget about shower games? After a word search puzzle, we did guessing games and anagrams before we tasted jars of baby food (gross!) and looked at diapers smeared with peanut butter (grosser!). Winners got prizes, mostly gag gifts. Daisy got a paper rose for being the oldest and the little girl got a bracelet for being the youngest.

At last it was time for food. Jewell brought out a tray of ham salad sandwiches, while Daisy and I carried in chips and dip, sliced fruit, cookies, and banana bread. I realized that, in the frenzy of preparations, I hadn't eaten anything since breakfast.

So I filled a plate for myself and was in the kitchen refilling my coffee cup when a young woman with curly red hair appeared and asked if I had any non-dairy creamer.

"Sorry to be a pain," she said, "but I'm allergic to milk. And I haven't yet learned to take my coffee black."

"No problem," I assured her as I began searching my cupboard. "I'm sure I have some powdered white stuff in here somewhere. It was Daisy's idea that we should have real cream—or half and half— or whatever that is on the table."

"This is a lovely house. It was so nice of you to take on Sarah's shower at the last minute like this."

"Well, Jewell and I are really good friends," I said as I handed her the container of non-dairy creamer. "And she was in a panic."

"My name is Crystal, by the way," the girl said as she spooned the powder into her coffee. "When my mother called and told me about the fire at the Pomeroy Inn, my first though was—oh, poor Uncle

Clint, but then my second thought was—oh dear, what about Sarah's shower."

"Well, I'm just glad that things have worked out—." Then I realized what I had just heard. "You said Uncle Clint. So are you related to Clint Pomeroy?"

"Sure. Uncle Clint is my mom's cousin."

"I see. Well, I've been trying to get in touch with him. But I've had no success. Guess he's been real busy since the fire."

"He is. We haven't seen him at all."

"Do you by any chance have a phone number for him—like a cell phone?"

"I don't, but my mother does. I could call her and get it for you."

"That would be great."

I wrote down my phone number for Crystal and was debating whether I should tell her that I was a reporter when I heard a scream from the living room. It was followed by a loud babble of voices with everybody talking at once. I pushed my way through the crowd until I found Daisy.

"What happened?" I said, grabbing her hand. "What's going on?"

"Oh, this is so exciting," said Daisy. "Sarah was in the bathroom and, well—it looks like—we think her water broke."

CHAPTER TEN

I left Daisy and made my way through the throng of excited ladies until I reached Sarah and her mother, who were in my bathroom having a heated discussion.

Sarah was in tears. "No, no, no."

"Just get in the car," said Jewell. "Cedar County Hospital has a fine O B ward."

"No, I want to go to Ann Arbor."

"That would take three hours. Anything could happen on the way."

"But the clinic has all my records—and I want Mark."

"We'll get Mark," Jewell said to her daughter. Then she looked at me and mouthed the words, *just leave us alone.*

"Let's give them some privacy," I said as I closed the bathroom door and tried to disperse the crowd. Finally the guests started moving into the dining room and a few of them sat down, but most of them continued to stand and talk, a few venturing to the kitchen for coffee refills.

After about ten minutes Sarah and Jewell emerged from their conference. Sarah's face was red from crying but her mother looked calm and determined.

Jewell made an announcement. "I'm taking Sarah to the hospital in Stanton," she said. "Tracy, will you come with us?"

"Of course."

"Good. Daisy, please stay here and look after our guests. Ladies, don't feel like you have to leave. Just relax and have some cake. Everything is going to be fine."

Shortly afterward, the three of us climbed into Jewell's car and were on our way to Cedar County Hospital.

"We should be there in twenty minutes," said Jewell. "Sarah, do you have your phone? Call Mark and tell him what's happening."

Sarah made the call, and apparently it went to voice mail because she left a message, telling him she was in labor and was on her way to the Cedar County Hospital. For her sake, I hoped that Mark was the kind of guy who checked his telephone messages frequently.

Sarah's distress was understandable. She had not expected to deliver her baby in a small town hospital. She expected to be in an up to date, state of the art clinic in Ann Arbor. She continued to sniffle and complain until she got a serious labor pain.

"Just focus on your breathing," said Jewell. And Sarah got quiet.

Jewell handed me her phone and had me call the hospital. "Tell them it's my daughter, she's in labor—and to have someone waiting for us with a wheel chair at the emergency entrance."

I did exactly as instructed and from the moment Sarah arrived, she received reassuring personal attention. She was, after all, the daughter of the hospital's director of nursing.

Jewell never left her daughter's side as Sarah was quickly admitted and whisked away to the labor room. I was relegated to the waiting room where I was soon joined by Paul. The two of us engaged in desultory conversation and leafed through worn magazines for a couple of hours until Mark arrived—much sooner than anyone had hoped or expected. Jewell came out and took charge of Mark. She offered constant reassurance while she dressed him in a paper gown and took him into the labor room.

So Paul and I continued to keep company in the waiting room, yawning and drinking coffee. It was dark outside when a nurse in scrubs appeared and told us that a healthy six pound girl had entered the world. Paul wrapped me in a celebratory hug and I swear I saw a tear roll down his cheek. Apparently he was so elated at becoming a grandfather that he forgave his not-quite-yet-son-in-law who was responsible for the event.

In any case, while Sarah was being transferred to her room, Paul encountered Mark in the corridor and the two of them engaged in some sort of manly hug. I have no idea what words they exchanged because I was distracted by the sight of a familiar figure moving down the hall in our direction.

Seconds later, I was engaged in my own hug with Frank.

"How on earth did you know we were here?"

"I stopped by your house and no one was home," he said. "I waited a little while and pretty soon Daisy came rushing over to share the news."

"Dear old Daisy. She is a bit of a gossip."

"You're not mad, are you?"

"Of course not. I'm glad to see you."

And it was true. In the excitement surrounding the blessed event, we both seemed to have forgotten whatever it was that we had been feuding about. Jewell came out of Sarah's room, looking tired but happy, and shared more hugs with everyone.

So there we all were—Paul and Jewell, Mark, Frank and I, when another nurse appeared, this one with gray hair and a serious looking cap and uniform. She assured us that mother and baby were fine but Sarah was tired and needed to rest.

"So you folks should just go and let her sleep. There are visiting hours tomorrow afternoon and evening." She glanced at Jewell for confirmation.

"She's right," said Jewell. "We'd better go."

The five of us headed toward the exit in a straggling caravan. Alternately we talked, laughed and then tried to shush one another. As we neared the door, Frank took my arm and said, "How about riding home with me?"

"How do you know I didn't drive?"

"Because your car is at your house, silly."

"Gosh, you must be a detective."

"Sometimes I get it right."

"Sure, I'd love a ride home."

So Frank and I went home together.

The next morning we were still in bed when the telephone rang, sometime around nine o'clock. After four rings, the answering machine took over. I heard Daisy's voice.

"Guess you two are not up yet," she said, sweetly acknowledging the presence of Frank's Blazer nestled next to my little Honda. "I'll just call Jewell instead."

"Do you think I should call her back," I said. "So she doesn't bother Jewell?"

"What I think," said Frank, "is that you should stay right here."

So I did.

It was nearly ten-thirty when we finally got up. We got out my skillet and made pancakes and sausage for breakfast. The phone rang again while we were eating.

"That's probably Daisy," I said. "I'd better take it this time."

I went into the living room and took the call—but it wasn't Daisy.

"This is Crystal," said the caller.

"Um, who?"

"Crystal. I was at the shower yesterday."

"Oh, right." I said, trying to remember exactly which one was Crystal. "Did you hear about Sarah's baby?"

"Yes, her cousin called me. We are all so excited." I wondered exactly why Crystal was calling, but didn't want to say so. She rescued me by coming to the point. "I just remembered—yesterday—I promised to give you Uncle Clint's phone number."

"Oh, yes—Clint Pomeroy. Do you have the number?"

She rattled off nine digits and I wrote them down. Then I felt obliged to share a few details about our evening at the hospital. "So thanks a lot," I said at last. "I've got company so I'd better go." She could infer whatever she wanted about my Sunday morning company.

I rejoined Frank and told him who Crystal was and why she had called me. "Marge wants a big follow up story about the Pomeroy Inn for this week's paper. Have you heard any rumors about arson?"

"Sure, but I doubt it's anything more than rumors." He refilled his cup. "Chief Jackson said it started in the laundry room and it could have been the clothes dryer. There's been a couple of cases with that same model dryer."

"That's good," I said. "I mean, it's bad enough the building had to go—it would be worse to think it was deliberate." I eyed the one remaining pancake. "Want to split it?"

"Sounds like a plan."

We shared the pancake and I drowned my portion in maple syrup. "About that body in the woods," I said. "Any news there?"

"Well, it looks like she's at least part Native American."

"Jake told me that."

"That's an educated guess—they haven't actually done DNA on her."

"So what are they basing this guess on?"

"Her features, her hair and a leather pouch she was wearing."

"Anyone can wear those."

"True. In any case we've started a computer search for missing person reports. There's a couple we're going to follow up, but the timing doesn't seem quite right."

"How so?"

"The closest one, geographically, is from up near Branch. A guy reported his wife missing. She was in her fifties—so the age was right—but the timing is not. He said she went missing in early March."

"Are you sure the body we found had been there all winter?"

"Definitely. That's how it looked to me and Benny—and that's what the post mortem indicated."

"So it couldn't be this guy's wife unless—."

"Unless she disappeared in the fall and he really took his time about making the report."

"If he did wait that long—wouldn't that look suspicious?"

"Yes—most guys would not take several months to notice that the wife was gone."

"You're right. They would notice when the dirty dishes and dirty clothes started piling up. So maybe he was the one who killed her."

"Possible. But those records are all in Lake County—so either Benny or I will be making a trip to Baldwin sometime soon."

"What was the other one?"

"That was over by Detroit. A man reported that no one had seen his mother since sometime last fall. They made plans for the holidays and she never showed."

"If you check that one out, you'll get to visit your old territory."

"Yep. But it seems like a fairly long shot. In the meantime, we've asked to have a forensic artist develop a sketch of what the victim looked like."

"How long will that take?"

"It all depends. Probably a week."

"Do you think Benny will want to run the sketch in the paper?"

"I think it would be a good idea—right now she's just Jane Doe. It's hard to solve a murder when you don't even know the victim's identity."

Frank hung around for the rest of the day. We drove to the beach and took a walk on the dunes, then visited Les and Daisy who, wanted all the details about Sarah and the baby. It felt good to be with Frank again. Since he didn't revisit the question of how Jake had managed to locate Benny and him in the woods, I didn't bring it up either. I figured it made sense to let sleeping dogs lie.

CHAPTER ELEVEN

Marge greeted me with a familiar question on Monday morning. "Have you found Clint Pomeroy yet?"

At least I had an answer this time. "No, but I'm making progress. I got a cell phone number from his niece."

"Then get on it and meet with him. I want to do a major feature on the family history of the Pomeroy Inn. And I need it by tomorrow."

"I'll do my best."

I went to my desk and called the number Crystal had given me. I got Clint Pomeroy's voice mail so I left my name and number with a polite request for a call back. I wasn't very hopeful but it seemed there was nothing more I could do, so I got busy tweaking the wastewater plant story from the previous week. To my surprise, I had a call shortly before noon, and the caller identified himself as Clint Pomeroy.

"I'm a reporter with the Shagoni River News," I said, "and I'm hoping you could spare some time to meet with me. We're planning a special story about the Pomeroy Inn. The whole town is in shock. The place was such an institution and—"

"Sure, sure," he said. "I'll be in town tomorrow."

"So could you—?"

"I've got meetings all day long. My lawyer, the insurance agent, my banker. Hell, probably even my dentist will want to see me. But I'm planning to lunch at the yacht club—."

"So, could I meet you there?"

"I guess you might as well come by and spoil my lunch. No reason it should be any better than the rest of the day."

This was the down side of my job. I hate pursuing people who don't really want to talk with me. But Marge had given me my marching orders. "I'd be happy to meet you at the yacht club," I said evenly. "It won't take long, I promise."

"Okay."

"What time would work out for you?"

"Around one o'clock—if everything goes as planned. But I may get tied up. I'll give you a call."

"Okay, thanks. You have my number, don't you?"

"I have it," he said. Then he ended the call.

So that was it. We had an appointment. But would he even show—or was he just putting me off? Hard to say. When I saw Marge, I told her I had talked to Pomeroy and we had scheduled a lunch meeting.

"Good work. How did he sound?"

"He sounded pretty grumpy."

"I've never seen him any other way."

So my interview with Pomeroy, if I managed to pull it off, promised to be a barrel of fun.

Tuesday morning I went to work early so I could wind up all my unfinished stories, leaving the afternoon free to work on the feature about the Pomeroy Inn—after I scored the interview with Clint Pomeroy. If I was so lucky.

I ate my lunch in the break room about twelve-thirty and decided not to wait for any phone call. I grabbed my writing gear and walked two blocks to the yacht club, where sunshine was bouncing off the little ripples in Arrowhead Lake.

I knew, of course, that one is supposed to be a member to even walk into the yacht club, but there wasn't any doorman around so I just ignored that rule. Inside, I saw two couples eating lunch by windows that offered a view of the lake, and a dark haired man alone at a table in the corner.

It had to be Pomeroy. He was turned away so I couldn't see much of his face, but I did see him open a container and shake something into his hand. It must have been a pill because his hand went to his mouth and he took a drink of water. Looked like maybe he had a headache.

I waited a beat and then walked across the room, stood directly in his line of sight and said, "Good afternoon, Mister Pomeroy. I'm Tracy Quinn, from the Shagoni River News."

"I know who you are," he said.

"Okay."

"You're the one who's sleeping with that cop."

"I guess my reputation has preceded me." If my private life was public, there was nothing I could do about that.

Clint Pomeroy was looking at me through a pair of dark rimmed glasses that made a dent on his bulbous nose. The bags under his eyes sagged into pouchy cheeks. I couldn't help but notice the obvious contrast between his grey moustache and suspiciously dark hair.

Pomeroy continued looking at me but said nothing more while he chewed on a bite of sandwich which was corned beef, to judge by what I saw on his plate. He motioned for me to sit down.

"Thank you." I took the chair opposite him.

"So what do you need to know?"

Clearly he wasn't about to waste any time on small talk. So I got right to it. "First of all, when was the place built? And was it built by your grandfather—or great-grandfather?" I stalled out for a second, trying to do the math in my head.

"No, no, no," he said, with in a dismissive gesture. "I'm not sure when it was built. Look it up somewhere. The place changed hands twice before my grandfather bought it—in the late fifties."

"So it wasn't always the Pomeroy Inn?" I had my steno pad out now and was scribbling furiously.

"No, my grandfather gave it that name—and made it popular. He died about twenty years later—in the seventies—and that's when my parents took it on. They made a decent living from the place until my mother died. That's when my dad got the bright idea that he would retire and go live in Florida."

"Did that work out?"

"Yes and no. Dad put the place up for sale. But after two years with no solid offers, I guess I felt sorry for him. I took out a bank loan and bought the place." He shook his head. "Here I was, trying to help the old guy out, and it's been nothing but trouble ever since."

"When did you take over?"

"About ten years ago. I sank a lot of cash into remodeling—but it turned out to be a huge waste of money."

"Why was that?"

He shook his head. "The heyday of the family inn was over. The state park came along and people were doing more camping—or they stayed in motels." He motioned to the waiter and pointed to his coffee cup. "And of course I had to pay a manager—I didn't have time to hang around and do that kind of thing. It was getting so that some years the place didn't clear enough to pay the mortgage."

The waiter appeared with a coffee pot and asked if madam wished anything. I debated for a minute and then motioned for him to fill my cup.

"So your dad moved to Florida," I said. "Is he still there?"

He shook his head. "Dad died a couple of years ago. I'm still trying to settle the estate. He had the poor sense to get remarried—then he and his wife both died at the same time. So now we've got to contend with her family and their claims on joint property. It's a royal mess."

Pomeroy had finished his sandwich and I was afraid I was going to lose him. But apparently he had ordered dessert, so I was saved by the arrival of a piece of cheesecake. The waiter asked me if I wanted some cake. It looked mighty tasty but I said no because I didn't think I had any cash with me. Besides, I needed both of my hands for taking notes.

Pomeroy dug his fork into the cheesecake.

"Your father and his wife—how did they die?"

"It was really stupid. You know, in those retirement communities, everyone drives around on a golf cart. That's what they were doing—but they took it off the grounds to go buy groceries and—got creamed by a truck."

"Oh—how sad."

"At least they went together. That's what everybody said at the funeral."

"Do you plan to rebuild the inn?" He had a mouth full of cheesecake and he didn't answer so I blundered on. "I mean, the place was insured, wasn't it?"

"Of course it was insured." He wiped the napkin across his mouth. "I'm meeting with my agent this afternoon."

"So—when the money comes through?"

"No way, never. I won't rebuild. Like I said, the hospitality business isn't working any more. When the place gets cleaned up, the property will still be worth a lot. I'll either sell it or develop it."

"Develop? As in condos?" The proliferation of condos in our historic village had become a hot button political issue.

His response made it clear that he was aware of that particular controversy. "Actually, I don't want to say anything about future plans. After all, it's much too soon to decide anything like that."

"Okay, fine. Here's what I'll say. How about, 'Mister Pomeroy is still dealing with the devastating loss of the family business and has made no decision about the future of the property'."

"That's good. Devastating loss—I like that. But don't make it sound like I inherited anything. I bought the damn place and I'm still buying it. The mortgage didn't go away just because the place burned down."

"But the insurance—hopefully it will be enough—."

He raised a hand to cut me off. "It would be nice if I got enough insurance money to pay off the bank. But you never know. Those goddamned agents are always looking for a reason to stall. Now they want their own fire investigation people involved."

"But isn't that pretty much routine?"

"Routine—crap. I know how they work. They drag their feet as long as they can before they pay out a single dime." He shoveled in the last bite of his cheesecake. "But don't put that in the paper."

"Of course not," I said. "I'll just use the stuff about—well, three generations of family owning it."

"Okay, I gotta go." He rose, threw down his napkin and headed for the bar where the young man was writing up his check.

"Thank you," I said to his departing backside. "Thank you for your time."

"No problem." Then he stopped and turned back to me. "Just remember what I told you not to print."

"I'll remember," I said, then jotted a few more notes before I walked up to the bar. I tried to pay for my coffee but discovered that Pomeroy had covered it.

"Well, that was very nice of him," I remarked to no one in particular.

"It's club policy," said the young man who was acting as waiter/bartender and cashier as well. "The member always pays for guests."

I walked outside thinking I should have ordered the cheesecake.

It felt so good to be out in the sunshine that I sat on a bench to review my notes while I watched a pair of sailboats glide across the shiny surface of the lake. I saw a woman launching her little boat from the dock and idly considered whether this would be the summer for me to take sailing lessons. But there was no time for dreaming. This was deadline day.

"Did you find him?" Marge demanded when I walked in.

"Got him," I said, with a wave of my steno pad.

"Okay, good. Try to finish by three-thirty so I can take a look at the piece."

The paper came out on Wednesday with my feature about the long history of the Pomeroy Inn. We used some old photos from the archives and Kyle had a story based on interviews with locals who had worked there when they were teens. I didn't hear from Pomeroy, so apparently I hadn't written anything that offended him. Either that or he didn't bother to read the paper.

The next morning I drove to Stanton and covered a special meeting of the county board which ended just before noon. I was on my way out of the courthouse when I saw Sheriff Dupree walking down the hallway toward his office. On a whim I turned around and followed him.

Dupree went into his office and I stood in the doorway, waiting for him to notice me.

"Oh, it's you," he said as he took a seat behind his desk.

"Are you busy?"

"No more than usual."

"I just came from the county meeting. They said there's some problem about, ah, who's going to enforce the county junk ordinance."

He shrugged. "It'll depend on the number of complaints. We'll have to wait and see how things play out."

"Okay thanks, and I was wondering—Frank said you had an artist working on a sketch of that woman—that body you found in the woods."

He nodded.

"So I was wondering—are you planning to run it in the paper?" Truth was, I wanted to get a look at it.

"It's not ready yet," he said in a tone that made me not believe him. I had known Benny Dupree long enough to know when he was stonewalling. I also knew when there was nothing I could do about it. So I thanked him for his time, said goodbye and got back to town in time to have lunch at the Belly Up Bar.

Frank called later, just as I was getting ready to leave work.

"How would it be if I brought something to your house for dinner tomorrow night?" he said. "I can get some take out."

"Sounds good. Can it be Chinese?"

"I'll be in Wexford. You'll have to settle for Mexican."

"Okay, that'll do. Remember mild sauce for me."

Frank was as good as his word. The next day when I got home from work, his Blazer was already parked in my drive. I found him sitting in my porch swing reading the newspaper.

"Did you get the food?"

"Sure. It's in the kitchen."

"Great." I sat down beside him.

He gave me a peck on the cheek. "Any plans for tomorrow?"

"Trying to talk myself into cleaning the garage. Want to help?"

"I've got a better idea. Let's take a trip to Manistee."

"Manistee? What's there?"

"The casino."

"Oh, the casino." Manistee was home to the Thunder Hawk Casino. "And what are we going to do there—besides drink and gamble?"

"Official business," he said. "Come on inside. I've got something to show you."

CHAPTER TWELVE

On Saturday, Frank helped me clean my garage. On Sunday, we had breakfast at my place before heading out on a day trip to the Thunder Hawk Casino.

"Ever been to the casino before?" Frank said as we entered Manistee.

"Never. How about you?"

"Couple of times. Back when it was new, we were up here deer hunting and decided to take a look."

"Guess you weren't impressed enough to make it a habit."

"Gambling just isn't my thing."

"I think the management prefers to call it gaming."

"Too bad. I call a spade a spade."

I twisted around so I could reach into the seat behind me and brought out a flat white envelope.

"Be careful with that," he cautioned.

"I am—I just want to look again. This isn't the original, is it?"

"No, it's a copy. But still."

I opened the envelop and slid out a piece of heavy paper, about four by six inches and covered with clear plastic wrap. I turned it over and a face appeared. It was a pencil sketch—the face of the murdered woman, as near as the artist could determine her features. I wondered exactly what he had to work with. Bones and hair and skin and teeth, I supposed—I didn't want to think too much about the condition of the body after it was unearthed.

The face the artist had rendered was nearly square, with a solid jaw and a strong nose. The dark hair was parted in the center and it was long enough to be pulled into braids on either side that were held in place with leather thongs. The artist had portrayed her thin lips as unsmiling, with a deep line running from the base of each nostril to the side of her mouth.

I stared at the face and wondered what secrets the woman had been hiding—secrets that might have led to her death. A small leather pouch hung around her neck.

"Was there anything in that pouch?" I said. Frank was silent. "Come on, you can tell me."

"I'm not supposed to say."

"You know I can keep a secret."

"Oh, all right," he said with a sigh. "It was nothing very helpful—just a little stone carving."

"A carving—of what?"

"A turtle. Which is a pretty common symbol for local tribes."

"For the Ottawa Indians?"

"You been doing your homework?"

"A little," I said. "The casino we are about to visit is owned by the Little River Band of the Ottawa people. Are you and Benny thinking she was a member of the tribe?"

"Maybe, maybe not."

"What would it mean that she was wearing the pouch and with stone inside?"

"Not a whole lot. Anybody can buy that stuff. There's a whole circuit of

powwows every summer with dozens of vendors. They sell stones, beadwork, wood carvings—anything you want."

"But she is Indian, isn't she?" I had momentarily given up given up on using the politically correct name. No one else seemed to use the term and it proved cumbersome, at least in conversation.

"Yes she is. Based on DNA from hair samples, she is at least half Native American. And that's why we are here." Frank slowed down and took a left turn off US 31.

"Do you think she may have gambled here?"

"I'm thinking more along the lines that she may have worked here. Or maybe there's a friend or relative working here. It's a place to start. And besides, it seemed like a nice day for a ride."

"Can't argue with you about that."

Though the morning had dawned cloudy, the sky was clear now except for a few puffy clouds. I put the sketch back inside the envelope as Frank made another turn and we entered the grounds of the Thunder Hawk Casino.

My first impression was big—a huge, sprawling building and multiple parking lots. Even the parking lots were big. "Take a look at those buses," I said. Four buses, the size of Greyhounds, sat off to one side, all of them decorated in gaudy colors that featured the Thunder Hawk logo.

"Those are the senior citizen buses."

"Really? All of them?"

"Sure. Well, probably any age can ride them. But it's mostly older folks who want to gamble but don't want to drive. The casino is kind enough to provide them with transportation."

"How thoughtful."

"I'm sure it pays off. Otherwise they wouldn't do it."

Besides the buses, there must have been over a hundred cars filling the lot near the building, but that left two more lots and the farthest one was empty. Frank maneuvered into the middle lot.

"Are you going to carry your purse?" he said after we were parked.

"I might. Why do you ask?"

"Thought maybe you could carry that picture for me."

"Let's see if it fits." I slid the envelope into my shoulder bag where it nestled between my wallet and my new digital camera. "Okay, just remember that I'm doing you a favor."

"In that case, how about if I buy lunch?"

"It's a deal."

We climbed out, then stretched and looked around before we started walking. We approached an entrance with large wooden doors surrounded by a stone façade which, even to my undiscriminating eye, was undeniably fake.

When we stepped through the doors, I felt as though I had been transported to another universe. This universe pulsated with hundreds of colored lights, all flashing in uncoordinated patterns that probably would have induced a seizure in anyone with epileptic tendencies. Row upon row of slot machines competed with one another for the gaudiest, brightest, most garish display.

Less than half the machines were in use. The machines that were occupied generally had a gray haired person sitting up close who methodically punched buttons and pushed coins as though feeding a hungry pet. Pictures of fruit, numbers, stars, and animals rotated constantly. A man playing was attached to an oxygen machine and a couple of women had placed themselves at the end of a row, the better to accommodate their walkers. High pitched, rhythmic music seeped in from above, suggesting the imminent arrival of a space ship.

After the slot machine area, Frank and I paused to watch a poker game where serious looking men sat at a table and frowned while they studied their cards. We passed an empty roulette table and I was tempted to reach over and give the wheel a spin. But I didn't.

We walked through a room with high ceilings where a fire was burning in a large stone fireplace. There were comfy looking chairs and a sofa in front of the fireplace, but no one was taking advantage of them. The rapid change of scene was making me a bit disoriented.

Frank brought me back to reality. "How about giving me that picture?"

"Okay." We both stopped. I reached into my purse and handed over the little package.

"Thanks," he said. "I think we need to go this way."

I followed him around a curve and into a lobby area which was bright with natural light from tall windows. Two people stood behind a counter of pale varnished wood. One was a young man and the other was a blonde woman no longer young, both wearing maroon uniforms and working at computers.

The lobby was filled with glossy signs announcing special hotel rates and upcoming concerts by entertainers I had never heard of. I stood back while Frank approached the counter. The woman had her hair in a French twist and her name tag said GILDA.

"Are you interested in booking a room?" she said.

"No," said Frank. "I'm just looking for information."

"Of course. How may I help you?"

"We're looking for someone." He showed her the sketch. "We're wondering—have you ever seen this woman?"

Gilda furrowed her brow and studied the picture for a moment. Then she shook her head and said, "No, she doesn't ring a bell with me. But I haven't been here very long."

"How long?"

"About five months."

"How about him?" Frank motioned toward the young man who was still at his computer.

"Jeremy," she said, "come take a look at this."

The young man came over to look at the sketch. He gazed at it briefly before he said, "Well she looks a little bit like Maureen—."

"Yes, but Maureen is a lot younger."

"Guess you're right," he said.

"How old is Maureen?" said Frank.

"About thirty. She'll be coming in at three."

"Okay," said Frank. "Thanks for looking."

"Sorry we couldn't help," said Gilda. "Are you looking for a missing person?"

"Yes, we are. So I'd like to speak to the manager. Is he available?"

"That would be Mister Greenwater. "Do you have an appointment?"

Frank shook his head.

"Let me check." She picked up a phone and punched some buttons. A minute later she said, "His assistant, that's Linda, said he should be here in an hour. And he can see you then—if you want to wait."

"Okay, we'll wait. Where's his office?"

"Just go down that hallway and turn left." Gilda pointed toward a corridor we had not yet explored.

"Fine," said Frank. "Where can we get something to eat?"

"There's food in the cafeteria. And the bar has food too if you would like to have a drink." She handed him a pamphlet which featured a map of the building. After a glance at the map, Frank and I left the lobby. Our route took us through a nature area with a huge skylight, waterfall and lots of potted plants. We peeked into the cafeteria and saw a line of elderly patrons shuffling past shelves that displayed sandwiches and salads in clear plastic containers.

"What do you think?" said Frank

"Doesn't look too appetizing. But I really am hungry."

"We can always try the bar."

"Food might not be any better."

"No, but we'd have something to wash it down with."

"Good point."

We took a left and headed for the bar. The place was nearly empty and we had no trouble scoring a table with a view of the waterfall. We drank beer with our hamburgers and I tried to imagine that we were on vacation in some tropical resort.

"You know what seems a little strange?" I said as I rescued a pickle that had fallen off my burger.

"What?"

"Well, I thought the place would be run by Native Americans." I kept my voice low. "But I haven't seen one yet, have you?"

"Only one—that woman who was checking ID in the gambling area."

"Guess I missed her."

"But you're mostly right. Almost every employee we've seen is Caucasian. But the Indian Tribe is the official owner."

"So the Indians hire the whites?"

"Looks that way."

I mulled this over while I finished my food. "When you go to see the manager, are you going to explain who you are?"

"Yes, I'll show him my badge and the whole works."

"And what about me?"

"I'll tell him you're my associate."

"Okay, I'll try to look professional."

"You look fine," he said. "There's just one thing you have to promise me."

"What's that?"

"No matter what happens, don't say a thing. Not a word."

"Okay, but why?"

"That way you can't get us into any trouble."

Until then, I had been happily enjoying the entire outing. It had never occurred to me that we might be stirring up any kind of trouble.

CHAPTER THIRTEEN

Frank and I finished our lunch and set off down a long corridor of the Thunder Hawk Casino. We were alone in the walkway which must have been the cultural education hall. An entire wall was devoted to large paintings that depicted North America's first inhabitants as they went about their daily lives; men making canoes or arrowheads, women harvesting corn or gathering berries with papooses strapped to their backs.

"Are you sure we're going the right way?" I said

"According to this map, we are."

"Guess you're right," I said a moment later. We had turned a corner and I saw a brass sign plate on the wall that read "Casino Manager." We walked through an open door into an office where a petite, dark haired young woman was working at a computer.

"May I help you?" she said.

"We'd like to see your boss," said Frank.

"Mister Greenwater?"

"Yes, if he's the manager here."

"Oh yes, he's the manager. Just let me check and see if he's busy."

She stood and walked to a door on her right, opened it and leaned in. A few quiet words were exchanged. Her voice was muffled but I thought I heard something about "two people we don't know."

The response must have been positive because she turned to us and said, "You can go right in."

Frank and I entered a large office and saw a man sitting behind a desk of polished wood, in front of windows that provided backlighting and created a halo effect. The wall to my left was hung with woven tapestries in zigzag patterns of gold, orange and green. The man stood to greet us.

"Come in, come in," he said. He came out from behind the desk to shake hands, first with Frank and then with me. "Welcome to the Thunder Hawk Casino. I'm Marvin Greenwater."

Our host was a tall man with black hair going gray and a lot of body mass that appeared to be settling around his belly. He wore a gray three-piece suit that contrasted nicely with a maroon shirt, and his string tie was held in place by a silver clip.

Greenwater favored us with a smile that did not reach his eyes and motioned to a pair of leather swivel chairs. Frank and I sat down and, when the man turned away, I saw that his hair was long, plaited into a single braid in the back.

"Would you like something to drink?" he said. "Coffee, water, tea?"

"No thanks," said Frank. "We just had lunch."

"Fine. I hope you ate here. And I hope everything was okay."

"Yes, everything was fine," said Frank.

Greenwater had been examining us from the minute we walked in. *did he think we were from the health department?* He leaned back in his chair.

"So—tell me who you are and what I can do for you."

Apparently the introductory dance was over and we were invited to lay our cards on the table—so to speak.

"I'm Frank Kolowski, a detective with the Cedar County Sheriff's Department. And this is my associate, Tracy Quinn." Frank pulled out his wallet and opened it to show his badge.

Greenwater was silent for a moment, leaning forward. Frank slid his wallet across the desk for inspection. The manager peered at it and said, "Cedar County. But we're not—"

"I know, I know. You're not in Cedar County—and of course I have no jurisdiction here."

"That's right."

"But I'm looking for someone." Frank took the sketch from me and passed it to Greenwater. "And since the person in question is

Native American, we thought we'd ask if she has ever worked here—or if any one here might have known her."

"Okay fine," said Greenwater, "that's fine. I always do what I can to co-operate with law enforcement."

"That's good to know."

Greenwater picked up the sketch but continued looking at us. "You see, when we first applied for permission to build this place, there were people who acted like the sky was falling—a gang of naysayers who claimed that a casino would bring in a crime wave. The fools insisted that a casino was synonymous with prostitution, robbery, drug dealing and murder."

Greenwater paused, possibly for dramatic effect. He still hadn't really looked at the sketch. "People like that just watch too many movies," he said. "It's been four years now and nothing bad has happened. Nobody underage drinks or gambles here. All we have brought to the area is steady jobs and good, clean entertainment."

"I have to agree," Frank replied. "I've never heard anything bad about this place."

"And we intend to keep it that way." Greenwater finally gave the picture he was holding a cursory glance.

"She was—she's not very tall," said Frank. "No more than five-two."

Greenwater continued to study the woman's face and then shook his head. "I can't say that I know this woman. Did you say she's missing?"

"Yes," said Frank, "since last fall."

Greenwater frowned, shook his head again. "Sorry I can't help you."

"Well, that's a copy," said Frank. "How about I leave it here and maybe you can show it around—see if any of your employees might have information."

"Sure, I'd be glad to."

"Here's my card," said Frank as he handed over a business card. "Don't hesitate to call me if you come across any information that might be helpful."

The manager took the card and laid it on his desk. He picked up a pair of coupons, stood and held them out to Frank. "Here, take these," he said as he handed them to Frank. "Entitles you to two free nights at our hotel—good for any time in the next two months."

"Well, thank you," Frank said as he took the coupons and slid them into his shirt pocket.

Greenwater glanced at his watch. "So—is there anything else I can do for you?"

"I think that's about it," said Frank. "Thank you for your time."

Greenwater walked with us to the door and again shook hands with each of us. As we walked by her desk, the secretary said, "There's a special show starting in the Jungle Room in about twenty minutes."

I thanked her and said nothing until we were well out of earshot, once again walking an empty hallway. I heaved a sigh and said, "What do you think? He was friendly enough, wasn't he?"

"Sure, but it's his job to be friendly," said Frank. "Especially with anyone involved in law enforcement of politics."

"You think he spread it on a bit thick?"

"Didn't you?"

"Yes, now that you mention it. I guess the reason I could never be a cop is that I'm not suspicious enough. But Frank, there's something I'm wondering about."

"Like what?"

"You let him think we were looking for a missing person—you never said anything about her being, well, murdered."

Frank glanced around to be sure we were still alone before he answered. "I wasn't sure how I was going to play it. That's why I told you not to open your mouth."

"And I didn't—except to smile."

"Right. Good job. You see, after Greenwater went through his long spiel about how law abiding everybody was, I decided that talk of a murder might make him turn all nervous and clam up—if he did know anything."

"Interesting. Do you think he knows something he's not telling us?"

"It's possible. What did you think of his reaction when I gave him the sketch?"

"Almost like he didn't want to look at it too close."

"That's what I thought too."

"So what does that mean?"

"Could mean something—or nothing at all. Maybe he needed his glasses and was too vain to reach for them."

"Hadn't thought of that. So what do we do now?"

Frank stopped and looked at his watch. "It's still early. Okay if we stay a while longer?"

"Okay by me—what are you up to?"

"I'd like to play some poker."

"Aha, so you do have the gambling bug."

"It's all research. Just want to get a feel for the place."

"Oh sure, research." We were now approaching the gaming area, with its low ceilings and flashing lights.

"So what about you? Want to hang around and watch me—or maybe play the slots?"

"Neither. I'm going to check out the Jungle Room."

"The Jungle Room?"

"Sure, why not?"

"Fine, have fun Want to meet in about an hour?"

"Sounds good. But don't come to me begging me for cash."

"Don't worry. They've got an ATM machine in here."

"These folks think of everything, don't they?"

"They really want us to have a good time."

Frank and I parted ways. I stood for a moment and watched as he disappeared into the den of flashing lights and high pitched music. Then I turned and walked to the nature area, where I sat down long enough to admire the myriad blue lights that were twinkling from somewhere in the depths of that waterfall.

There were plenty of signs directing me to the Jungle Room and once I made the final turn, I joined a straggling crowed headed for the same place. Most of the crowd were women on the far side of fifty, making me feel like a veritable youngster. I heard one of the women let out a squeal just before she stopped, whipped out her camera, and snapped a photo of a man with a pompadour dressed in a white jumpsuit. Then she handed the camera to her friend and stood with the man, who put an arm around her for another photo.

That's when I knew I was very close to my destination. Not only was Elvis in the building, he was performing this very afternoon in the Jungle Room. The show had already begun when I slipped inside and found a seat at a table with several women and one man who looked as though he would prefer to be someplace else. Before much time had passed, I realized we were not only seeing Elvis, we were seeing several different incarnations of him.

First a young Elvis came on stage, wearing a suit coat and dark slacks, as he gave us a stirring rendition of "Heartbreak Hotel" and "Love Me Tender." At the end of each song, the room erupted into a round of enthusiastic applause. Then the guy did "Blue Suede Shoes" and made his exit dancing.

I managed to score a glass of wine from the bar before the next performer appeared, this one an Elvis in striped prison garb who sang "Jailhouse Rock," complete with dance steps. When he disappeared, there was more wild applause until an Elvis with collar length hair appeared, wearing black leather and crooning "Are you Lonesome Tonight". This time he introduced the pelvic motions that had made him famous.

Finally a roar went up as Elvis in the sequined white jumpsuit came on stage singing, "Can't Help falling in Love with You." The performer glided through his repertoire of songs, some I knew and a few that I didn't, until he finally ended with "How Great Thou Art." The religious tune seemed a little out of keeping with all the bumping and grinding that had preceded it, but the audience didn't care. The applause was prolonged and hysterical.

By this time I wasn't sure how many different performers had swiveled across the stage. That question was answered when three men came out and took their bows together. There were cries from the audience begging for encores but the trio had apparently been advised to leave the audience wanting more. Because the audience, of course, needed time to go out and do some gambling. The performers disappeared and the announcer came out to tell us that there would be another show at seven p.m.

I looked around and wondered which women in the audience were hard-core fans who would spend three hours gambling while they waited for the next show. I knew for sure that I wasn't one of them.

I made my way out of the Jungle Room and found Frank waiting for me.

"Sorry if I'm late," I said as I took his arm.

"No problem. Just finished up myself."

"Any luck?"

"I did okay," he said with a bit of a smirk. "But I'm going to quit while I'm ahead."

"Well, aren't you the smart one."

"Ready to head back? We could stop for supper in Ludington."

"Either that or pick up a pizza and eat it at my house."

"That would be even better."

As we left the building, we had to detour around a bus marked "Casino Express," which had pulled up to the portico. A queue of elderly passengers was lined up to board for the return trip. Guess they weren't going to see the second Elvis show.

A few minutes later we were in Frank's Blazer and on our way home. We talked for a while about our impressions of the casino but then we both fell silent, a situation that was not unusual for Frank and me. Neither of is the kind of person who feels the need for constant conversation.

But then I noticed something strange.

We were south of Manistee when Frank's driving became erratic. First he speeded up, well over the speed limit, although there was no one in front of us for him to pass. I didn't say anything, but then he slowed down until it seemed like we were crawling—no more than forty I'm sure.

I started to wonder if there was something wrong with the vehicle—or worse—if there was something wrong with Frank. So while I usually make it a point not to question anything he does, I finally couldn't help myself.

"What's with your driving?" I said. "First you were speeding, now you're crawling."

He was quiet for so long that I thought he was ignoring me—which I don't like. "Don't turn around," he said at last, "but take a look in the rear view mirror."

"Okay." I leaned sideways and did as he had directed.

"See that gray sedan behind us?"

"I see it."

"I think the guy is tailing us."

"You think so?"

"I'm pretty sure."

I peered into the mirror at the image of the car and its driver. Near as I could tell, it was a man and he was alone in the car. "How long has he been behind us?"

"Ever since we left the casino."

CHAPTER FOURTEEN

Suddenly our springtime drive in the country didn't feel quite so idyllic. If Frank was right and the guy was tailing us—well, we were heading for my house. Whoever our stalker might be, I didn't like the idea of him knowing where I lived.

"What are we going to do?" I said.

"Got a pen and paper?"

"Of course," I said as I reached into my purse. "Reporters are always prepared."

"Okay. We are going to get his license number. Focus on the last digits, and I'll get the first part."

"How are we going to do this?"

Frank didn't answer. Instead he slowed even more, then suddenly pulled off onto the shoulder of the road and stopped. The car was forced to go past us and I was ready with my pen, paper and eagle eyes.

We remained parked on the shoulder while we compared notes on the license plate. Michigan plates use a combination of numbers and letters. I thought it was 60L and X92 but Frank said the first part was 6CL.

"It was easier when they were all numbers," he said. "But we'll just run it both ways. Keep an eye out for him now." Frank let a couple of car go past us, then proceeded to pull back onto the road.

"Do you think he knows?" I said.

"Unless he's really dumb, he must realize that we spotted him."

"So he'll give up, I hope."

"I hope so too. But I'm thinking—let's go into Ludington—drive around, maybe down to the lake, and then find some place to have dinner."

"Sounds nice. Are you getting all romantic on me?"

"I'm always romantic. But I don't want this guy tailing us back to Shagoni River. I don't want him to know where you live."

"We could go to your place."

"Now there's a thought. No way he could be inconspicuous following us down that two-track to my cabin on the river."

"He'd probably get stuck and you'd have to rescue him."

"That would blow his cover for sure. But I'm pretty hungry. Let's go to Ludington and drive around see if we can lose him. That way he won't be able to find either one of us."

So that's what we did. I kept my eyes peeled for the grey sedan but didn't see it again as we drove into Ludington and then through downtown all the way to the beach. We parked and got out. Behind us was a grassy area with picnic tables. In front of us was a broad expanse of sandy beach bordering Lake Michigan. We started walking across the beach.

Not a whole lot of people were around, but four teen-age boys were in the water, yelling and jumping as they carried on a game of Frisbee. By the time we reached the waterline, I had sand in my shoes so I stopped and leaned on Frank while I took them off. I poked an exploratory toe into the water and it confirmed what I already guessed. The lake was nothing but recently melted ice. Frank kept his shoes on. From time to time he glanced back toward the road.

"See anything of our friend?" I asked as we headed back.

"I saw one that might have been him, but the car didn't stop—at least I don't think so."

"He could have stopped down at the far end to wait for us."

"He might have done that. This road is all one-way."

Frank didn't say anything more about the stalker but, after we got buckled in, he made a U-turn and blatantly broke the law by driving the wrong way and leaving through the park entrance.

"Oh, you wicked man," I said when we had safely merged with the traffic on Lakeshore Drive. "What would you have done if a cop had stopped you?"

"Guess I would have tried to explain my situation."

"And he would have thought you were delusional."

"Good chance. But I have my identification——."

"Oh sure, and your girlfriend to back you up."

"Anyway, if that was our guy, he's still waiting for us down by the exit."

"And will be for quite a while."

"So where would you like to have supper?"

"Jewell told me about an Italian place she liked."

"Let's try it."

We had dinner at a restaurant called Luciano's where we drank red wine and listened to a guy playing classical guitar. Frank filled up on ravioli and I had the perch special, despite some long ago warning I had heard about avoiding fish at an Italian restaurant. The meal left me with no ill effects.

It was after seven when we left Ludington.

Frank suggested that we stop to see Paul and Jewell. "I told Paul I would help him get his boat in the water, but that was two weeks ago—so I don't know if he still needs me or not."

"Sure, that's a great idea."

I welcomed the suggestion because I had not seen Jewell in person since the night she became a grandmother. She had called me several times—once to thank me for hosting the baby shower—then to give me an update on the baby's eating habits—and the last time had been to tell me she was using her days off to drive to Ann Arbor to see the new family.

Of course I understood, more or less. Since I had never become a mother, I would certainly never be a grandmother, but clearly it was a milestone in her life and I knew that her absence did not represent any threat to our friendship. Even so, I had missed our time together.

Frank turned off Arrowhead Highway and followed a winding road through the woods for a couple of miles. He made the turn into

Lavallens' driveway and I was pleased to see two vehicles, indicating that both Paul and Jewell were at home.

In short order, the four of us were seated on their deck, drinking coffee and eating Jewell's strawberry rhubarb cake. The sun was sliding toward the horizon, splattering the lake with shades of crimson and orange on its way down. I couldn't help but notice how the friendship between Jewell and me had attained a nice symmetry now that men in our lives had found common ground.

As it turned out, Paul still needed Frank's help to launch his boat and they worked out a time for that project. That settled, Jewell indicated that she and Paul had news they wanted to share.

She looked at her husband and said, "Can I tell them or do you want to?"

"Oh, you go ahead," he said.

Jewell beamed. "Mark and Sarah have set a date for their wedding."

"That's great," I said. "Will she be a June bride?"

"No, they need more time. They've settled on the last Saturday in September."

"So—where will it be? The venue I mean."

"They've started looking. It depends on what's available."

"Too bad the Pomeroy Inn is gone," I said. "That place hosted a lot of weddings."

"That family is nothing but a bunch of crooks," Paul said with a derisive snort.

"What Paul means," said Jewell, "is that I made a deposit for the shower—and it doesn't look like I'm going to get it back."

"I hadn't thought of that. Have you talked to anyone about it?"

"I tried calling their business number but, no surprise, it's out of service."

"I guess I could give you a number for Pomeroy's cell phone. But—." I stopped short, remembering the interview.

"But what—?"

"I talked to Clint Pomeroy Monday, for the paper, and he was barely civil. Plus he was crying about money."

"That's about what I guessed," said Jewell. "He'll be in no mood to write anyone a refund check."

The two men started talking about fishing again so Jewell and I stacked the dishes and took them inside. "Is Paul happy about Mark and Sarah?" I said. "Now that they've set a date?"

"I'm sure he is, though he reserves the right to be grumpy about the prospect of a baby at the wedding."

"He'll get over it, I'm sure."

"And he's already started grumbling about what the wedding will cost and who is going to pay for what."

"I know what Paul needs."

"Good. Tell me."

"He needs to get his boat in the water and go fishing."

Jewell laughed. "Maybe you're right."

"Since I've moved here, I've noticed there's some kind of magic about hunting and fishing. It seems to give the guys an escape from their daily routine, and they come back with a new perspective."

"Nice theory. I hope you're right."

"And now the really important question, Jewell. What are you going to wear? For the wedding, I mean."

"Oh that. I do have the black chiffon. I've only worn it a couple of times."

"No way. No black for the bride's mother. You and Sarah need to go dress shopping."

"Good idea. But you should come along."

"Nice of you to offer, but I'm not known for my taste in clothes. Ivy is the clothes horse." I regretted that comment the minute it slipped out, by passing my internal censor.

"Well, I certainly don't want Ivy on my shopping trip."

"Of course not. Sorry I even mentioned her."

"Well, enough about me." Jewell deftly changed the subject. "What did you and Frank do this weekend?"

"Believe it or not, we just came back from the casino."

"The casino? I didn't take Frank for a gambler."

"He's not, at least not very much. But there was somebody up there he needed to talk with. So I just went along for the ride."

Suddenly I wondered if I was revealing too much about Frank's work, which was an ever present hazard of our relationship. I was relieved when Jewell didn't push me for any details. She had heard about the body in the woods, of course, but the issue was not in the forefront of her mind—that space was obviously reserved for Sarah, the baby, and the upcoming wedding.

I also didn't breathe a word to Jewell about the man in the grey sedan who had followed Frank and me when we left the casino. There was no reason to cast a pall over our visit. It was late when Frank brought me home so we shared a good night hug on the porch.

"You're not worried about that guy, are you?"

"No. I mean, I don't think so."

"I can stay overnight if you want me to."

"That would make me feel safer," I said with a giggle. "But I wouldn't get enough sleep. So thanks, but no thanks."

"Okay," he said. "Just be sure to lock your doors."

After Frank left, I tried to put the stalker incident out of my mind. But I couldn't help thinking about it, especially after I had gone to bed, only to lie awake with the whole thing running through my mind like an endless loop.

Who was the man? What did he want? Was he through with us— or did I have to keep one eye on my rear view mirror, always on the lookout for that mysterious gray sedan?

CHAPTER FIFTEEN

I woke up with sunshine pouring through my bedroom window, but the light felt more like an intrusion than a cheerful promise of things to come. I hit the snooze button, rolled over and went back to sleep. When the alarm went off again, my brain was working enough to tell me that it was Monday morning and getting up was non-negotiable. So I rolled out of bed and downed some orange juice and toast.

As soon as I got to work, I followed the scent of freshly brewed coffee into the break room. I poured myself a cup and was about to leave when my escape route was blocked by the appearance of my boss, Marge Enright. Marge was wearing a blouse I had never seen before—it had a swirling pattern of red and black and was accompanied by red plastic earrings.

I was not quite prepared, either for Marge or her new outfit, and decided not to comment on her latest look. Marge never seemed to appreciate compliments anyway. We exchanged cursory greetings and I was hoping she wouldn't ask me anything about my weekend. She didn't.

"Don't forget," she said. "You need to be in Stanton by ten o'clock."

"Of course," I replied, combing my brain for data while I tried to act like I knew what she was talking about. The data wasn't forthcoming so I finally gave up. "Um, what for?"

"Did you forget? It's that public hearing "

"Oh that. Of course." But I still couldn't remember much. It was Monday morning, for heaven's sake. "What's the hearing about?"

Marge gave me her special look reserved for idiot employees. "It's about the county-wide junk proposal."

"Oh yes, of course." And this time I did remember. "One of the commissioners told me it's looking to become a big issue."

"It could be a bit contentious. Everyone I've talked to seems to have a strong opinion, one way or the other."

"I guess this could be an interesting morning."

Marge left and headed toward her office. I went to my desk and tried to finish a piece I was writing about the Women's Club Flower Show. But I got distracted when I heard Marge talking to Jake in the hallway. There was something about running a picture in the paper—and what page it should go on.

I waited until I saw Jake go into the break room and then decided I was in need of a refill. Basically I ambushed him. "Got a minute?" I said.

"Sure. Come in my office."

I followed Jake into his office. "Have you seen the sketch of the Indian woman?" I said.

"Yep, Sheriff Benny gave me a copy so we could run it in the paper. With a request for information if anybody knows anything."

"And what does Marge say?"

"She's okay with the plan except she doesn't want to put it on the front page. I'd like to see it on the top half of the front page. Some people only look at the paper on the newsstand and they don't buy it unless something catches their eye."

"Good point."

"Have you seen the sketch?"

"Yes, I have. Frank and I went up to the casino Sunday and showed it to a few people, asking if they had ever seen her."

"Do any good?"

"Nothing yet. But we left a copy. Hopefully it will get passed around."

Jake motioned for me to close the door. I closed it.

"I talked with the sheriff this morning," he said. "Benny thinks he's got a lead—with a missing person report over in Lake County."

"You mean the one near Stony Creek?"

"That's the one."

"But I thought that woman went missing in January."

"Benny went up and talked with the guy. The story was that she left last fall to visit her sister in Texas. Then the husband left too—went out west to go bear hunting. He didn't expect to hear from her because neither of them had a cell phone. But when he got back home, he did expect her to call—you know, the holidays and all—but she never did. He called the sister in Texas but the sister said she had never arrived. That's when he reported her missing."

"And this woman is Native American?"

"He says her father was."

"Sounds like a possibility."

"Yes, and there's another thing."

"What?"

"She used to work at the casino."

I had a lot to think about as I drove the ten miles to Stanton. If this was our woman, then wouldn't someone at the casino have recognized her? But Jake didn't say how long ago she had worked there. Maybe there was a lot of staff turnover. We didn't even know how long Marvin Greenwater had worked there—although he talked as though he had been there from the beginning.

The courthouse parking lot was full when I arrived, so I mumbled a few choice words at no one in particular. I wondered if there was an especially juicy trial going on that had brought all these people to town at ten in the morning. If so, it seemed like I should have known about it.

When I finally found a parking spot, it was two blocks away, but the walk was no hardship. In fact, the hike improved my mood a little since no one with a pulse could fail to be uplifted by the bird song issuing from the maple trees on the court house lawn.

Once inside, I realized that it wasn't a trial that had drawn so many people to town. Marge had been right. They were all here about junk. In the county board room, the seats for the general public were already filled and more than a dozen people were standing. That was fine with me—lots of people with lots of opinions made it easy to write a good story.

The crowd was largely male and the ages ranged from forty to senior citizens. Some were in overalls, others in camouflage and a lot of them wore rubber boots, a dead giveaway that they were farmers who had to deal with the muck and mud that are an integral part of spring in rural Michigan. The commissioners, six men and one woman, were already seated at a horseshoe table in the front of the room.

As politely as possible, I worked my way through the crowd to the press table. Most of the group gave way when they recognized me as reporter for the local paper. This was one of the perks of the job, I had discovered—it carries a bit of clout. No one wants to get on the wrong side of the press.

I was not the only reporter to show up for the event.

Ivy Martin was already seated at the press table. Ivy is my fashionable friend whose artistic makeup and colorful scarves always make me think I am looking not quite right for whatever occasion we are both attending. Ivy is smart and funny, with a good nose for news, and I have always enjoyed her friendship. Always, that is, until the unfortunate incident with Jewell's husband.

Ivy had moved on. First she took up with a lawyer who moved in with her and stayed through most of the winter. But that was over now, because the lawyer had been arrested for kidnapping and murder. I wondered how long it would take Ivy to replace him. She spent a lot of time complaining about the lack of eligible men, but she never stayed alone very long.

"Tracy," she gushed as I sat next to her. "So good to see you. It's been ages."

"Yes, it has," I said, though I was pretty sure our last meeting had been less than two weeks before.

Ivy's gold earrings flashed as a ray of sun shot through the windows. "I've had a development in the romance department," she whispered. "Do you remember Steven?"

"Um, Steven who?" My attention was divided as I struggled to keep my pen and notebook on the table while I tore open a manila envelope and pulled out a stack of documents.

"Steven Quinn, silly."

The papers slid out of my grasp and onto the floor.

As I bent to pick them up, I struggled for an adequate response. Of course I remembered Steven Quinn. He was my ex-husband.

CHAPTER SIXTEEN

Ivy's news about a romance with my ex-husband had me baffled and a little intrigued. But we didn't have a chance to pursue the subject. The board president called the meeting to order, ending our conversation. What followed was a heated discussion of old machinery, unlicensed junkyards and the rights and responsibilities of property owners.

About an hour into the meeting, Ivy slipped me a note that said, *let's have lunch at schooners?*

Two hours later, when the meeting finally wrapped up, I was hungry and also curious enough to accept Ivy's lunch proposal. She had left the table and was engaged in conversation with the board president. I needed to get a quote from the Redfield Township Supervisor so I hurried to catch him in the hallway. But I left a note on the table for Ivy that said *see you there.*

Twenty minutes later, the two of us met up at Schooners Bar. Shortly after that, I began to regret my decision. We were seated at our favorite corner table and Ivy was babbling nonstop about her new romance.

"I'm just so excited. Steven's promised to come for a visit, maybe in a couple of weeks, and we're going to rent a cottage on the beach. We want to have a beach party and—of course—I'm hoping you and Frank will come."

At this point Ivy must have noticed my lack of response and also, perhaps, my dumbfounded expression. She looked at me with a critical eye and said, "You're not jealous, are you?"

The waitress arrived with our food, which gave me time to consider Ivy's question and put together an answer that would not sound like it came from a bitter ex-wife. "I really don't think I'm jealous, Ivy, but the fact is, I just prefer not to see the guy."

"Well, you should be over him by now." She pulled out her compact, flipped it open and studied her reflection. "I really don't like this shade of mascara," she said, apropos of nothing. Her features took on a familiar, pouting expression. "Besides, in case you don't remember, you are the one who gave me his e-mail address."

Had I really done that? and if so, why? Steven had been out of my life for well over ten years and I would have been happy to have things remain that way. He changed his residence so often that most of the time I had no idea where he was anyway. That had been the comfortable state of affairs until last winter when he showed up at my place, uninvited and unannounced, to see if I could help him get in touch with his daughter.

I had been more than a little upset to find my ex-husband in my house and that is probably why, as a sort of peace offering, Steven had offered to buy me dinner. I remembered taking him to the Antler Bar, one of the few businesses in town that stayed open through the winter.

"That night when you introduced us at the Antler," Ivy said, "I just felt like we had a connection."

It seemed to me that Ivy tended to *feel connections* with any man who still had a full set of teeth. But I didn't say that. What I said was, "Ah yes, but weren't you living with Greg Wetherell at the time?"

"I was. But then—you know—that all fell apart. It came as a terrible shock when Greg threatened to kill me."

"Yes, it surprised all of us."

"But eventually, when I recovered, that was when I remembered meeting Steven and I remembered what beautiful eyes he had—"

Oh yeah, Steven and his soulful eyes.

The waitress stopped by to refill our coffee cups and ask if the food was okay—maybe because neither of us had eaten a bite so far. So I dug into my tuna sandwich, eager to get through this encounter as quickly as possible. Ivy ate one bite of her chicken salad and then resumed talking.

"So remember, that day after a board meeting I asked if you had an e-mail address for Steven—."

"Yes, so you did." I remembered that I had actually felt a bit sorry for Ivy at that point in her life because she was without a boyfriend—and for her that constituted a full scale emergency. Providing her with an e-mail address had seemed like a fairly safe thing to do. But now it seemed that my action had born unforeseen consequences. Steven was coming to town??

I couldn't feign much interest but Ivy didn't seem to notice. She continued her blow-by-blow account.

"After you gave me his address, I sent Steven an e-mail. It was just a short note and I said that maybe he wouldn't even remember who I was—but—surprise, surprise, he answered the very next day. With a nice long message. We wrote back and forth for almost two weeks until I gave him my phone number. Ever since then, we've been talking on the phone—lately it's been almost every day and sometimes we talk for an hour or two. He's just so smart and funny.

"And now," she sipped her coffee as she paused for dramatic effect, "now Steven has some time off and wants to come and see me."

I smiled in spite of myself. Given what I knew about Steven, the fact that he had free time probably meant he'd been fired from his latest job. But I didn't know this for a fact and saw no reason to burst Ivy's bubble. Certainly Ivy didn't need any warnings from me about Steven's record with women. She was hardly a novice when it came to affairs of the heart.

Ivy was talking more than she was eating so I finished my food well ahead of her. With a glance at my watch I said, "Sorry to cut this short, but I have to get back to the office. Do let me know how things turn out."

But Ivy wasn't ready to let me go. "Wait a minute," she said, as she leaned across the table, her voice lowered to a conspiratorial whisper. "Is there anything about Steven that—well, anything I should know?"

So now I was supposed to share girl talk with her? "He's not a physical abuser," I said, thinking that the bruises Steven inflicted had all been invisible. "He's not a serial killer or anything like that."

"Oh, of course. But that's not what I was thinking of. I was wondering more about,"—the conspiratorial whisper again—"how is he in the bedroom?"

Had she really said what I thought she said? Now I really wanted to get away. I glanced around the restaurant, noted the crew of construction guys arriving. I was standing with my purse in hand. I leaned down close to her and said, "Umm, nothing kinky. Nothing to worry about." And with that I turned to leave.

She grabbed my hand to stop me. "But in general, I mean, performance wise, how would you rate him?"

No one had ever asked me a question like this before. But it was clear that Ivy would not let me go until she had an answer. "Probably a B minus," I said as I jerked my hand away and made my escape.

That ridiculous conversation replayed in my head on the drive back to Shagoni River. Once again I wished there was some way I could just avoid Ivy's company. But as long as she had her job and I had mine, we would have to see each other.

There had been times when I considered looking for another job, but had quickly discovered there was nothing I could do that didn't involve a long commute. Besides, being a reporter had turned out to be good for me. Although I'm not the outgoing type, the work assignments had forced me into contact with the movers and shakers in the area. I was beginning to feel a real connection with my adopted home town.

For once I was glad to get back to the office. Things were busy enough that I didn't have a chance to think any more about Ivy and Steven. I managed to write up my story about the junk meeting, using lots of opinionated quotations from various officials. The piece was fairly long but I knew that Marge would feel free to cut it down if she ran out of space.

After work, I swung by the grocery store to buy some fresh asparagus. I had never thought much about the vegetable until I moved to Michigan, but I had never eaten it really fresh either. At home, I cooked the asparagus while I reheated some leftover mac and cheese. It made a good supper and I'm sure it contained every vitamin and mineral that I needed.

After supper, the daylight was so persistent that I felt I should try to accomplish something. So I stacked the dishes, changed into my grubbies and headed for the garage to see if I could coax the lawnmower into starting up for another season. I was almost out the door when the telephone rang.

It was Frank.

"Hi, it's me. Okay if I stop by?"

"Sure—how soon?"

"About five minutes."

"So where are you?"

"Down at the marina."

"You're not buying a boat, are you?"

"Just looking. I don't think I can afford one right now."

"Not unless you get lucky at the casino. Sure, come on over."

Frank arrived and I went out to meet him. We walked up to my porch and sat together on the front steps, swatting the occasional mosquito.

"What have you been up to?" I said. "You look like you might have some news."

"Am I really that transparent?"

"That's because I'm getting to know you."

"Well, it's not a huge breakthrough—but I did run the plates on that guy."

"The one who followed us from the casino?"

"Yes, him. The car is registered to a Lyle Mardeen."

I thought for a moment, shook my head. "I've never heard that name. Do we know anything about him?"

"A little," he said. "On further snooping I discovered that Mardeen is employed by the Thunder Hawk Casino—as a security guard."

"Aha. So it looks like Greenwater sent him after us. But why do you suppose he did that? What was the guy supposed to do?"

"Maybe he wanted to scare us off—or maybe it was just to worry us a little. It's possible he wanted to know if we were who we claimed to be."

"If Greenwater is so worried, then I wonder if he's guilty of something."

"Kind of looks that way. But there is one other possibility."

"What's that?"

"Maybe Greenwater didn't send him. Maybe the guy had his own reasons for following us."

"But I don't see how—?"

"Remember, after we showed the picture around, we still spent a few hours at the casino. So the news of our search for a missing person could have been circulated."

"So by the time we left—."

"By the time we left, Lyle Mardeen might have heard about us and decided to stick his nose in."

"So maybe he was the one who wanted to scare us off."

"If that was his plan," said Frank, "it had exactly the opposite effect. Now I really want to go back to the casino so I can snoop around a little more."

"I'm not sure I want to go with you this time."

"Why not? We've got coupons for the hotel."

"Hmm. Do you think the hotel has a pool and hot tub?"

"I'm pretty sure it does."

"In that case, I'll consider another visit." I said. "Have you had supper?"

"Yes, already ate. You need help with anything?"

I nodded in the direction of the garage. "I was about to do battle with my old lawnmower."

"Let's see when we can do."

Frank went to the garage with me and filled the gas tank on the lawnmower, then checked and added oil. After that he yanked the rope and the motor coughed but didn't start.

"Darn," I said. "That's when I was afraid of. This mower belonged to my grandpa and it must be a hundred years old."

"But it ran last summer didn't it?"

"Yeah, somebody helped me get it running."

"Then it's too soon to give up." He started looking through a dusty shelf lined with even dustier cans that contained motor oil, weed killer, wiper fluid and some unidentified substances. He picked up a can and said, "Here's what you need—starting fluid—it works every time."

"I forgot about that."

Frank shook the can, bent down and aimed it at a shiny cylinder near the motor. The can emitted a misty spray that smelled like ether.

"Now let's see." Frank pulled the rope and the motor coughed to life.

"It's a miracle," I said. "Last week I looked into hiring a lawn service and the prices nearly gave me a heart attack."

"Let's take it out for a run," he said. So Frank mowed the lawn while I ran interference, picking up stray branches and other dangers that lay hidden in the fast growing grass. We finished the front lawn in less than an hour.

"Just use that starting fluid every time," he said as we stowed the machine in the garage.

"Thanks. Somebody told me that last year but I forgot all about it. In any case—I think you've earned yourself some chocolate cake."

"My favorite. Did you bake?"

"No, but Daisy did and she brought over a very generous chunk."

"Got any ice cream?"

"Let's go look."

The ice cream was chocolate ripple and Frank declared the combination perfect. We sat on the porch to eat our dessert. The lowering sun flashed on the wings of scissor-tailed swallows as the birds swooped across the lawn in search of insects for their evening meal. Afterward, we took our dishes to the kitchen and I found a bottle of wine. We took the wine to the living room along with a pair of glasses and settled down on the sofa.

"There's something I need to tell you," Frank said as I poured the wine.

"Uh oh. This sounds kind of serious."

"Nothing to worry about. I just wanted to let you know that I'm going to be gone for a couple of days. Looks like I'll head for Detroit tomorrow morning."

CHAPTER SEVENTEEN

Frank's announcement should not have come as any surprise.

Since we'd been together he'd made more than several trips out of town as part of his work, but this time the news made me a little uneasy. Maybe it was because of this Lyle Mardeen person who had followed us from the casino. But I didn't want to come across as fearful, so I didn't say anything about my misgivings.

"Are you going to check out that other missing person report?" I said.

He nodded. "I kind of volunteered for it. It'll give me a chance to see my daughter and the boys. I can spend the night with them and save the cost of a hotel."

"So you'll get to see your grandchildren."

"Yep. I missed a birthday last month so maybe I can make up for it."

"Better bring a present."

"I will. Any suggestions?"

I thought for a moment but came up empty. "You should know more about boy stuff," I said. "Some kind of truck or one of those ugly toy monsters."

"I always wanted a chemistry set."

"Well there you go—a chemistry set." I kicked off my shoes, took a sip of wine. "Do the kids know what your job is?"

"The older one knows. He thinks I'm like one of those detectives on television."

"Guess the reality is not quite as glamorous."

"Certainly our cases don't get solved in an hour."

"When you were growing up, did you always want to be a detective?"

"As far as I can remember, I just wanted to grow up."

"And now you have. Just think—you're a grandfather already. And I will never be a grandmother."

"Somehow that just doesn't seem fair." He pulled me close.

But then, in the midst of a steamy kiss, I had a thought which made me pull away. "Frank," I said, "I heard a rumor about that woman—."

"What woman?"

Did he think I was suspecting him of infidelity? "I'm talking about the dead woman in the woods."

"Oh, her."

"Yes, that one. I heard that the cause of death was strangulation. Is that right?"

He nodded. "Her hyoid bone was crushed so that's a pretty good indication."

My hand flew to my throat again. I imagined the victim struggling for breath, her face turning blue. Then I remembered the picture of her—and that pouch hanging from a strip of leather around her neck. "Was it that leather thing around her neck?"

"We don't think so."

"Why not?"

"It didn't seem strong enough. It would have broken before it killed her. There were some shreds of rope near the body so that was probably the murder weapon."

"Such a terrible way to die."

"If it makes you feel any better, she probably wasn't conscious when it happened."

"How do you know that?"

"The toxicology report showed Xanax in her blood stream."

"So she was taking Xanax. Isn't that an anti-anxiety medication?"

"Yes, but this was a huge overdose, enough to make her unconscious."

"So that means—what?"

"It means she was drugged before she was killed."

I thought for a moment. "I guess that makes me feel a little better—but not much. She's still dead."

"Yes, somebody definitely wanted her out of the way. But remember—don't talk about this. To anyone."

"Of course. Have I ever let you down?"

"Yes, once. Not too long ago."

"Oh come on. Are you still chewing on that?"

"I probably shouldn't. It wasn't your fault that Jake managed to find us."

"Good. I guess we never really resolved that."

I was afraid he might ask me where I had heard the rumor about strangulation but fortunately he had other things on his mind. Frank kissed me again and after that we didn't talk for a while. It was after dark when he finally left.

Jewell called the next day to remind me about our book club meeting.

"I thought maybe we could have dinner first," she said, "at the Mexican restaurant."

"That's fine with me. Do you think Fiona will want to join us?"

"I think so. I'm going to call her next."

"She's kind of dropped out over the last few months."

"She had a lot going on in her life."

This was true. Fiona, a nurse who worked with Jewell, had been widowed the previous winter. First she had been a suspect in her husband's death and, after that was cleared up, she had been forced to deal with her step-children. The two daughters who came home for their father's funeral had pretty much moved in with Fiona.

"You see more of her than I do," I said. "How do you think she's holding up?"

"She seems to be fine, considering all she's been through."

"Are Charlene and Rose still living with her?"

"Charlene found a boyfriend and moved in with him. I'm not sure about Rose. Hopefully Fiona will give us an update tomorrow."

"Great."

"And, I'm not sure about this, but I've heard rumors that Fiona might be seeing someone."

"Seeing someone—as in dating?"

"That's the scuttlebutt."

"Any idea who it might be?"

"No, not a clue."

"Seems a bit soon, doesn't it?"

"Who are we to judge? I don't think the marriage was a very close one."

The next day Marge assigned me an out-of-town interview. I was to do a piece about a guy in Ludington who was heading up the area's first ever triathlon. I didn't even know what the word meant until Marge explained that it was a race involving three modes of locomotion. In this case, the contestants would begin with swimming, then they would bicycle, and finally run. It was hard for me to understand why anyone would undertake such punishment, but a number of athletic types from Cedar County were already signed up.

As I drove north in my little red Honda I tried not to think about Lyle Mardeen. After all, we'd been in Frank's blazer when he followed us, so Frank was the one he was after. Certainly not me. I managed to forget the whole business until I was driving down Ludington Avenue and thought I spotted a grey sedan behind me. But, after I took a left turn, I didn't see the car again. Clearly I was suffering from an overactive imagination.

I parked in the lot behind the chamber of commerce building. Inside I was met by the aptly named Mel Trotter, who was president of the triathlon committee. Trotter was in his mid thirties with—no surprise—a lean, athletic build.

The interview was easy. The man was totally psyched about his project and basically couldn't stop talking. After an hour I told him I had enough information and thanked him for his time. He loaded me up with pamphlets and application forms for the race, gave me his cell phone number, and told me to call him any time.

I said goodbye to Mr. Trotter and went outside where I found my car, unlocked the door and slipped in. Throwing my purse aside, I dropped the papers on the passenger seat and turned back to close my door. But I couldn't close the door because, all of a sudden, somebody was in the way.

I let out a little yelp when I saw him. A tall, skinny guy had managed to sneak up on me and was standing with one arm on my door and the other on the roof of my Honda. I struggled to quell my fear, telling myself it was probably just a bum who was going to ask for money. But he didn't really look—or act—like a panhandler.

"Please let me go," I squeaked. "I'm in a hurry."

"Just wait a minute," he said. His voice was soft but hoarse, like someone who's had throat surgery.

I took a deep breath and glanced around in search of a helpful bystander but there was no one in sight—plenty of cars, but no people. I turned the ignition key. The engine started but the guy didn't budge.

"What do you want?" I did my best to sound calm as I craned my neck to look up at him. Most of his face was hidden behind sunglasses and a scruffy beard.

"I'd like to talk with you."

"And who are you?"

"My name is Lyle Mardeen."

CHAPTER EIGHTEEN

"You've been stalking me," I said to the stranger who was holding me hostage in my own car. "And there are laws against that." I tried to sound indignant rather than terrified.

"Look, I just want to tell you something. About that woman."

"What woman?"

"The one you two were looking for when you came up to the casino."

Bingo. So maybe this guy knew something. But I wished mightily that Lyle Mardeen had managed to track down Frank instead of me. I wished that I could call Frank and tell him to get his butt up here so he could hear what this guy wanted to tell us. But Frank was in Detroit and I was on my own.

A lot of thoughts raced through my mind. First of all, I knew that I wanted to hear what this guy had to say—whether it was the truth or not. And maybe being a detective was not that different from being a reporter—it was all a matter of collecting information. So I ought to be able to handle this myself.

But one thing I knew for sure—I didn't want to pursue a conversation with this creepy stranger in a deserted parking lot.

"Let's meet down at the coffee shop," I said, thinking he couldn't do me any harm if we were in a public place.

"I'd rather talk you right here."

I proceeded to pull my door closed. "Meet me at the coffee shop."

"How do I know you won't just drive away?"

I sighed, exasperated. "If I did, you'd just tail me again."

He said nothing.

"Look, I promise. Let's meet there in ten minutes."

"Okay." He slowly moved away so I could close the door of my car.

Relieved, I pulled out of the parking lot and had to deal with a very strong urge to flee the scene. But my stronger impulse was to find out what he had to tell me. *Could this be the guy who had killed the woman? Well no that didn't make any sense. But maybe he knew who did—or at least he knew something about the casino that we didn't know.*

I drove downtown and scored a parking spot right in front of the Daily Grind Java Shop. It was the last empty space on the block so I figured Mardeen would have to park behind the place and, when he arrived, would come in through the back door.

I went inside, got a coffee and took a seat with a good view of the interior. I kept my eyes on the back entrance. Three girls came in, talking loudly, and minutes later they were followed by a pair of middle-aged women. That's when I started to wonder if maybe Lyle Mardeen had stood me up.

Well damn. Here I was so sure I was going to come up with a gem of information to pass on to Frank. And wouldn't he be impressed with my sleuthing abilities? But now it looked like I had let the guy get away because—because why, exactly? Because I was afraid to talk to him in broad daylight in downtown Ludington?

Then a figure appeared off to my right, almost behind me

"Hey there," he said in that same soft, strained voice. Lyle Mardeen had fooled me by coming in the front. I glanced at him and tried to appear unsurprised.

"Hi," I said as I motioned to the chair opposite me.

Mardeen sat down and leaned forward, putting his elbows on the table. He slid the sunglasses off his bony nose and looked at me from deep set watery eyes.

"Do you want coffee?" I said.

He shook his head. I waited, but still Mardeen said nothing. Just sat there and looked at me.

"Okay then." I took a deep breath. "I know you work for the casino. So what was it you wanted to tell me?"

He bit his lower lip before he answered. Finally he said, "I saw that picture you guys brought up to the casino. The one of the missing woman. And I'm pretty sure I did see her once—sometime last fall." The way he stretched his vowels made me think he might have grown up in the south.

"Okay—but when did you see the picture?"

"The same day you were up there. Greenwater's secretary made some copies. She brought one of them to the employee lounge and told us that you folks were looking for a missing woman."

"Okay. When was it you saw the woman? Do you know her name?" I was tempted to reach for my notepad but didn't want to do anything that might make him clam up again.

"I don't know her name. But I reckon I saw her—probably in October."

"At the casino?"

"Yes. The hotel had expanded. They ran an ad for housekeeping staff for the new wing. She came in and talked with the head of housekeeping."

"Was it about a job?"

"That's what I thought, but I don't know for sure."

"Why didn't Greenwater tell us this?"

"He probably never saw her. Lenore's the head of housekeeping. If Lenore wants to hire someone, then Greenwater gets involved. Apparently she didn't get hired."

"Why didn't she get hired?"

"No idea."

"Okay—but why did you follow me and Frank? Why all the sneaking around?"

"Because Greenwater doesn't like anybody going behind his back. He doesn't want anyone else talking to the law. Wants to do it all himself."

At that point I realized that Mardeen probably thought I was what Frank had said I was—a plainclothes cop or detective. I wasn't about to enlighten him.

"Well, you have certainly put a lot of effort into finding us."

He shrugged. I worried that maybe the guy was some kind of nutcase with too much time on his hands. I took a small notebook out of my purse and jotted down some notes.

"I guess we need to talk with Lenore. Can you tell me her last name?"

"Her name is Lenore Cooper. But she doesn't work there any more."

"Why not?"

"I dunno. She quit right before Christmas. Kind of sudden."

I laid down the notebook and looked across the table at my informant. I tried to think like Frank. "This may be helpful," I said. "I will certainly share it with my partner. Could you please give me your address and phone number?"

Mardeen hesitated briefly before providing me with his cell phone number. And a PO box number in Manistee. I knew that Frank wouldn't think much of the PO box as an address, but I figured we could catch the guy at work if we needed to.

"Is there anything else you'd like to tell me?"

I took a sip of coffee while I waited for an answer. He shook his head.

"Well thank you," I said. "And I hope I won't see your car behind me any more."

He smiled for the first time, showing crooked teeth. "Nope. Just wanted to let you know about that."

Lyle Mardeen stood and disappeared out the front door. I sat for a few minutes, and made some more notes, just as I would have done if I were writing a newspaper story. Then I finished my coffee and drove back to town.

As soon as I reached the office I called Frank, eager to tell him about my big scoop. The call went to voice mail and I asked him to call me right away. But there was no response as I spent the rest of the afternoon writing up the piece about Mel Trotter and the triathlon.

By the time I got home from work, I started having doubts. Maybe Lyle Mardeen was a pathological liar and nothing he had told me was true. Maybe my big scoop didn't mean anything at all. I tried again to call Frank and once again left him another message. This time I told him I had met with Mardeen and had a talk with him. Then I did my best to put the whole thing out of my mind.

While I was waiting for Jewell to pick me up, I remembered what Ivy had told me about her romance with my ex-husband. Now that I was through being surprised about the unlikely development, the whole thing struck me as pretty hilarious. Normally I would have been eager to share the laugh with Jewell. But if I did, I would be breaking my own rule again—the rule about avoiding any mention of Ivy.

By the time Jewell pulled up in front of my house, I had decided to keep the news to myself. From the minute I climbed into her car, we had plenty of other things to talk about, especially now that a baby granddaughter had joined the family. Ten minutes later we breezed into the restaurant, which was just beginning to fill up with the supper crowd.

"Fiona usually gets here before we do," said Jewell.

"There she is," I said as I spotted the wild red hair that identified our friend Fiona Crawley, who was already sipping a Margarita. Fiona was pushing fifty, but her remarkable hair and generous smile made fools of men half her age.

Fiona waved to us. When we joined her, she stood to share hugs with both of us.

"There you are," she said, "my two life savers."

When the waiter appeared, Jewell and I ordered quickly, since we pretty much had the menu memorized. Fiona already had chips and guacamole on the table.

"Here, dig in," she said pushing the chips in our direction.

As we munched and talked, Jewell lost no time in producing baby photos and Fiona pored over them making appreciative comments.

My mouth was full of chips when Fiona turned to me and said, "Tracy, I heard something and I wonder if it's true."

I swallowed hard, took a drink. "I'll enlighten you if I can."

"What I heard," said Fiona, "is that Ivy is involved with your ex-husband."

I nearly choked on my wine. *So much for not talking about Ivy.* "And where, exactly, did you hear that?"

"From Ivy herself—at the grocery store. I was trying to grab a couple of things in a hurry but she collared me and spent much too long bending my ear about this wonderful guy she was seeing. Or going to see. Or some such thing."

Too late now to spare Jewell's feelings. I glanced at my friend to see how she was taking this, but Jewell wasn't showing any visible reaction. I couldn't suppress a smile as I visualized the grocery store encounter. "Don't believe everything you hear," I said. "I mean about what a wonderful guy he is."

"Of course," said Fiona. "We all know that Ivy tends to dramatize her romantic life. But do they—or do they not—have something going?"

"Oh, they probably do," I said, "and the sad part is that it's mostly my own fault—for passing on his e-mail address."

"Has she ever met him?" said Fiona. "In person, I mean."

"Yes, for about five minutes last winter."

"Wow. I guess she must have been really impressed."

"I think it's more like Ivy is really desperate. For her, life without a man is an emergency situation that needs immediate first aid."

"Well, I guess she found someone to give her CPR," said Fiona. We both burst into giggles and Jewell started laughing too.

"But there's more," said Fiona. "Before I could get away, Ivy invited me to a bash she's giving when he comes to visit. She said something about a beach party."

I glanced at Jewell again and decided that she was okay with this exchange. She seemed more amused than anything else.

"Ivy does tend to be a busy girl," said Jewell.

The waiter arrived with our food and for several minutes we were occupied with the distribution of sour cream, dressing and salsa. The taco salads and enchiladas were far more interesting than Ivy's latest romance.

I was starting on my second shrimp taco when Jewell said to Fiona, "How are things at your house? Are Rose and Charlene still living with you?"

"I'm living alone and loving it," she replied. "Remember Charlene met that strange guy in town who is such a good friend of her brother? She moved in with him. So I guess those two have something going."

"What do you think of the guy?"

"My honest opinion is that he is a loser—but so far not abusive. That's the most we can ask where Charlene is concerned."

"And what about Rose?"

"Rose has gone back to California. She likes living there, plus she wants to keep an eye on her mother."

"Her mother who just got out of rehab?" I said.

"Yes, and she seems to be doing okay."

"What a lot of drama. So is your life getting settled down?"

"Slow but sure. You see, Vince had talked about making a will— but when he died, I still didn't know if he had ever got around to it. I never saw the will, never had a copy. But a couple of days after the funeral, I got a call from Joel Dukes."

"Joel Dukes, the lawyer?"

"That's the one—so I made an appointment with him. And a week later, me and all three kids went trooping into Dukes' office to hear him read the will."

"I thought that only happened in movies," I said.

"Or with very rich people," said Jewell.

"Well, this wasn't a movie," said Fiona. "And Vince did not fall into the category of very rich. But he wanted his son to have his truck and snow plow. That was fine with me because snowplowing is one of the few ways Chip has of earning money."

"So what about the girls?"

"He left his car to Charlene and that was good because she really needs one. But he left nothing to Rose because she seemed to be doing okay on her own."

"That hardly seems fair."

"I know. That's why I gave her—well—a sum of money. It was just about enough to get her back to San Francisco and keep her afloat while she looks for a job."

"Generous of you."

"I did my best. And I'm not hurting—because we had just paid off the house. She smiled at Jewell. "Plus I've got a good job—and a really great boss."

Jewell smiled. "How was Joel Dukes to deal with?"

"Very helpful," said Fiona. "Turns out I had met Joel a couple of times before when he brought his dad to the emergency room."

"Oh, now I remember him," I said. "Joel Dukes brought his father to Daisy's wedding."

"Yes," said Jewell, "and the poor man died in her living room."

"As it turned out," said Fiona, "I'm really glad that Joel was the person I had to deal with."

"He's a good guy?"

"He is," she said. "But not only that—he also happens to be single."

"Aha," said Jewell, "so the rumors of a new boyfriend are true?"

"That's a bit of a stretch," said Fiona. "We are proceeding with utmost caution. So far, just a couple of lunch dates. But I like the man, I really do."

CHAPTER NINETEEN

When I got home from the book club meeting, the message light on my phone was blinking. The message was from Frank and he asked me to call him. But before I could do that, he called me. We spent only a few seconds on small talk before he posed the question that was on his mind.

"Tell me what happened with Mardeen," he said.

"I was in Ludington doing an interview," I replied. "My car was in that parking lot behind the chamber building. I didn't see anyone when I came out and got in my car, but he sneaked up on me and blocked me from closing my door."

"So he was he tailing you?"

"He must have been."

"How did he get from following my car to following yours?"

"I have no idea."

"Damn. I don't like that."

"Believe me, I didn't either." Now I was feeling like I had done something wrong. *Why did I let Frank do that to me?* "All I know is that he was there. I figured if I drove away he would just follow me again, so I told him to meet me in the coffee shop."

"Good move. So what did he—?" The rest of Frank's sentence was drowned out by static.

"Frank, I can't hear you."

"You're—breaking up. " His words came out garbled. "—home tomorrow. Call—then." So much for the wonder of cell phone communication.

"Okay," I said, "call me tomorrow." Of course I had no idea whether he heard me or not.

In any case, I felt relieved just to know that Frank would soon be back in town. I still couldn't help getting a little nervous every time I saw a grey car behind me. But so far none of the cars I had seen resembled the one belonging to Lyle Mardeen. Besides, he had promised to quit tailing me—but what did that mean? I didn't know the guy and had no idea whether a single word that came out of his mouth was true.

As promised, Frank called me the next day. I was at work, getting ready to go to lunch. "I'm in Stanton," he said, "and things are pretty busy around here. Can I come over tonight?"

"Sure, that would be great. I'll even cook dinner."

"That sounds good. I'll bring ice cream."

I wanted to ask him what he had found out in Detroit, but I saw Marge moving in my direction so I said goodbye. My curiosity would have to wait until I saw him in person.

Had I really offered to cook supper? I must have been carried away. What on earth was I going to make?

I had never been a gourmet cook, but I did pick up some basics from my mother and, later on, my grandmother. Then came marriage. My husband had greeted all of my culinary efforts with such sarcastic criticism that, by the time we divorced, I was reluctant to cook for anyone other than myself. Frank, with his omnivorous appetite and appreciative comments, was doing his best to allay my kitchen insecurity.

I decided to rely on that old standby, spaghetti.

After work, I swung by Lorenzo's grocery store where I grabbed a cart and tossed in some onions, ground meat and a jar of pasta sauce. I was headed for the checkout when I saw a familiar figure coming in the door. It was Ivy Martin, who currently topped the list of people I really didn't want to talk to.

Since Lorenzo's is not very big, the situation required some adept maneuvering on my part. I turned back and lurked in the frozen food section until I could no longer see Ivy and then I made a bee line up to and through the checkout. Fortunately there was no one else checking out and I sailed through pretty fast. I was breathing a sigh of relief as I headed toward the door. That's when I heard Ivy calling me.

"Hey there, Tracy," she said, "wait up a minute."

But I kept moving. "Sorry, gotta run," I said as I gave her a half-hearted wave and made my exit.

I broke into a little trot on the way to my car, just in case Ivy had decided to follow me. After I pulled out of the parking area, I scolded myself for acting downright silly. Perhaps it was immature of me to go to such lengths to avoid Ivy. But damnit, I just wasn't ready to listen to her getting all mushy about my ex-husband.

By the time I reached home, I had forgotten all about Ivy and was busy thinking about supper. I carried in my groceries, checked the mail and got busy in the kitchen. I had a bad moment when I couldn't find the spaghetti—I was so sure I had a box that was nearly full—but I finally found it lurking behind the toaster.

I put a pot of water on to boil, chopped some onions and garlic. I browned them in the skillet, then added the sauce and started looking for some seasoning. I was trying to decide between curry and chili powder when I heard a knock at the door.

"Come on in," I yelled.

"Sure smells good in here," Frank said as he walked into the kitchen. He put a grocery bag on the table and I turned around just in time to get wrapped in a big bear hug.

"You smell good too," I said. "Oops, careful." I was holding a wooden spoon, which came close to dripping tomato sauce on both of us.

"Shucks, it's not a spaghetti dinner if you don't get some of it on you." He kissed me on the cheek. "And look what I brought."

Frank let go of me and reached inside the bag, producing a carton of ice cream and a bottle of wine. "Is it red wine that goes with spaghetti?" he said.

"Darned if I know. I never managed to learn about what goes with what. But I'm sure that bottle of merlot will work out just fine."

The water in the pot had started boiling, so I handed Frank the wooden spoon and told him he was in charge of the skillet. I dropped spaghetti into the boiling water and threw together a salad. Frank finished the sauce while I drained the spaghetti and then he poured us two glasses of wine. We lost no time in getting the food onto our plates.

"Okay now, tell me about Mardeen," he said as soon as we were seated.

So, while we ate, I told him every detail I could remember about the man who had stalked me until we finally sat down and had a conversation at a coffee shop in Ludington.

"Somehow it just doesn't make sense," said Frank.

"Maybe not. But Mardeen said that when he saw that sketch of our missing woman, he remembered seeing her come to the casino—just once. And he followed us because he wanted to tell us about it."

Frank frowned. "Do you think that he was telling the truth?"

"I don't know. I'm not very good at spotting liars."

"He certainly must have had a pretty strong motivation. He put a lot of time and effort into following us—and then finding out who you were and chasing you around."

"Now that I think about it, I'll tell you one thing that struck me."

"What's that?"

"The way he talked about Greenwater—it was almost like he resents the guy—and sort of enjoyed going behind his back."

"It's very possible that he does. A lot of people don't think too highly of their bosses."

"And I wonder about the housekeeper who supposedly talked to the mystery woman. Why did she leave—and what happened to her? It seemed like a good lead, but now it's another dead end."

"Well, not a complete dead end. You've got her name—right?

"Lenore or Lora something like that—last name Cooper."

"We can try to find her."

"If we could—then we could show her the sketch and see if she remembers the woman. Hey, I just had another idea."

"What's that?"

"If the woman was looking for a job, wouldn't she have filled out some kind of application form?"

"It seems more than likely. In any case, there's one thing I know for sure."

"And what is that?"

"We need to make another trip to the casino—and we might as well use those coupons and stay at the hotel. This time I'll talk with Mardeen instead of Greenwater." He pushed away his empty plate. "And by the way—dinner was excellent."

"You can take some credit for that," I said.

"Because I stirred the skillet?"

"And brought the wine. Shall we have dessert in the living room?"

"Definitely."

I poured two cups of coffee while Frank dished up the ice cream. We moved into the living room and cleared clear space on the coffee table for our final course.

"Now tell me about your trip to Detroit," I said.

"It was good. I got to see my grandsons. Jimmy's eight already. My gosh, those kids grow fast."

"That's nice, but what about that lead you were chasing—the guy who reported his mother missing?"

"Oh, that."

"Did you find him?"

Frank punctuated his answer with a disgusted snort. "I spent a couple of hours driving through some pretty grimy back streets before I located him." He shook his head, took a drink of coffee.

"And?"

"He was half in the bag in the middle of the afternoon—at a strip club."

"Sounds like fun."

"Those places are pathetic." He shook his head. "Anyway I finally got him talking and the whole thing was a fiasco."

"How so?"

"Remember, this was the guy who was worried about his mother—afraid something had happened to her."

"Right. How old was he, anyway?"

"Forty something, maybe—hard to tell—drunks trend to age early. I think she had been living with him and what he really missed was her social security check."

I laughed. "Did he ever find her?"

"Yes he did, but then he neglected to inform the police."

"And where was dear old mama?"

"Living in Florida. She went down for a vacation where she met—and married—a charter boat captain. She never told her son because she didn't want him coming down to freeload."

"So he lost his mama and her pension check?"

"Yes, and here is the really sad part of the story."

"You mean it gets worse?"

"From his point of view, yes. Because the new husband—he showed me a photo of the happy couple—and the new husband looked to be younger than the guy I was talking to."

"That's a good one. More power to her."

I was at home the next evening when Ivy Martin called me. When I heard her voice, it became clear that I was about to have the conversation I had been postponing. But I figured it would be easier to deal with her on the phone that it would have been face to face.

"I really wanted to talk with you at the store the other day," she said, "but you—well—you just ran out of there like you were on your way to a fire."

"Sorry—but I was in a hurry." I remembered that the best lie is built around a kernel of truth. "I had promised to cook dinner for Frank and I was running late."

"Well never mind. I'll just have to share my news over the phone. Steven called yesterday and he is definitely coming to visit. He's already got his plane ticket."

"Oh."

"And he'll be here next weekend."

"That's nice."

"And, like I said, we're going to throw a party. I've already rented a cottage on the beach. We're going to have a cookout, fireworks, plenty of beer, and of course I want you and Frank to come."

"Ivy, I'm not sure—I'll have to talk to Frank. I think he said something about—um—about going out of town next weekend."

Ivy continued to chatter about her plans with Steven but I wasn't really listening because suddenly a couple of things started lining up. Finally I said, "Okay Ivy, I won't keep you any longer," as though I had been the one who called her. "I'm sure you have a lot more people to invite."

As soon she was off the line, I called Frank.

"Hey," I said, "how about we make that trip to the casino next weekend?"

"Next weekend would probably be okay. Any special reason?"

"Yes, in fact, there is a reason. I'll tell you about it when I see you tomorrow. "

Our Saturday plans involved a visit to the Lavallens. Frank was going to help Paul put his boat in the water. And once the men had made their plans, Jewell insisted that I come along so the four of us could have dinner at their house.

Frank was supposed to pick me up around five, but it was closer to six when he arrived. "I called Paul," he said, "and told him I was running late."

"I guess it's not much of a problem when we have daylight for another four hours."

"That's what I love about spring. It's payback for our suffering through the dark days of January."

As I climbed into the Blazer I said, "Frank, do you have those coupons from the casino with you?"

"I think so." He pulled a bulging wallet from his pocket and handed it to me. "You find them."

As we headed for Arrowhead Drive, I sorted through his cash and trash until I found the two coupons. I straightened them out and read them carefully. "Okay, each one says, 'Good for one night for one room for up to two people.'"

"Yep."

"Well, we don't want to stay two nights, do we?"

"Wasn't planning on it."

"Great—so let's invite Paul and Jewell to go with us. They can use the other coupon."

"Sure, good idea. So what's the big deal about next weekend?"

"Oh that. I need to get out of town because Ivy invited us to a party at a cottage she is renting on the beach. The party is to celebrate her newest boyfriend—who happens to be my ex-husband."

Frank took his eyes off the road to glance at me. "Did you say your ex-husband?"

"That's what I said."

"As in the one who showed up at your house last winter?"

"Yes, Frank. I only have one ex-husband."

"Sounds a bit complicated."

"That's putting it delicately. In any case, it's not a party I want to go to."

"Me neither," he said. "What a good time to go to the casino."

"Great idea."

We pulled into Lavallens' yard and discovered Jewell working at one of her flower beds. She put down her trowel and came over to greet us. Right about then, Frank spotted Paul down at the boat dock, waved to him and headed toward the lake.

Jewell took my arm and we started into the house. "You won't believe the phone call I had today," she said.

"Maybe not. But try me."

"Ivy called and invited us to her party next Saturday."

"You're kidding," I said, stopping in my tracks. "I don't believe it."

"See, I told you. But it's true."

"My god, what nerve. What did you say to her?"

"Nothing. Fortunately it was just a message on the machine."

"Did you tell Paul?"

"I haven't yet. Think I should?"

"Absolutely not." We resumed our walk into the house and, when we got inside, I said, "Besides, you and Paul have plans for next weekend."

"We do?"

"Yes, you do. This is working out just perfect."

"What do you mean?"

"Frank and I have a freebie for overnight at the casino—and it's for four. You and Paul have been selected to join us—next Saturday night."

"Is this for real?"

"This is definitely for real. So whatever happens at Ivy's party—we won't even know about it. We'll be miles away—having a good time."

CHAPTER TWENTY

"Did you remember my electric shaver?" said Frank

"Yes and your toothbrush too. They're in my overnight bag."

Frank and I were in his Blazer on our way to the Thunder Hawk Casino and so were Paul and Jewell. But the four of us were not together.

"Tell me again why we're traveling in separate cars," he said.

"Mainly because Jewell thought it would work out better that way."

"And why was that?"

"She wants to be back home Sunday afternoon in case Mark and Sarah are able to visit. And I figured you wouldn't want any time constraints if you manage to track down Lyle Mardeen."

"You're right. Because I'm planning to do that on Sunday."

"Why not today?"

"Because, as near as I can figure out, Marvin Greenwater works on Saturday—but as a rule, he's not around on Sunday."

"Which should make things much easier for you."

"Right. What time is the dinner theatre business?"

"Seven o'clock I think."

"Want to get a bite to hold you over?"

We were driving through Manistee, which had the usual array of fast food choices. The suggestion was tempting because my hasty lunch had been nothing but a bowl of lentil soup. But I resisted.

"I'd like to save my appetite for dinner," I said.

"Fine with me."

"Since we're paying dearly for the dinner, I'd like to get my money's worth." As it turned out, that was a decision I would live to regret.

We had arranged to meet up with Paul and Jewell in the casino parking lot and found them already there when we arrived. The four of us went inside and made our way through the room full of blinking slot machines to the lobby, where the check-in process went along without incident.

Apparently the desk clerk was accustomed to seeing the complimentary vouchers that we presented. We bought tickets for the evening entertainment, which was a dinner theatre production called Tony and Tina's Wedding. Minutes later, we were in an elevator on our way to rooms 302 and 304.

Frank used the key card to open room 302. It was a fairly large room with two double beds, two armchairs, a desk, a television, a microwave and a counter with bottled water, cups, and packets of instant coffee or cocoa. I pulled back the curtains on the window and found that we had a view of a parking lot, but beyond that were trees and more trees. We parked our overnight bag on one of the beds and plopped down on the other.

"Pretty good mattress," said Frank.

"Not bad. But what's that smell?"

"I think it's the carpet. They smell like that when they're new."

Frank and I were debating whether to give the bed a workout when the telephone rang. It was Jewell. "Can we come over?" she said.

"Sure. Come on over and we'll decide what to do next." I smiled at Frank and shrugged as I hung up the phone.

"Apparently married couples don't feel the urge to check out hotel room mattresses," he said as we proceeded to rearrange ourselves.

"I hope we didn't interrupt anything," Jewell said as she and Paul entered the room and found us sitting on the bed.

"No problem," I said. "We've got a little over an hour to look around the place."

"Ever been here before?" said Frank.

They both shook their heads.

"Then let's start by going downstairs for a drink."

"Sounds like a good idea," said Paul.

"The bar's pretty nice," I said. "It's close to the nature area with a waterfall and all kinds of tropical plants."

Frank had to refer to his complimentary map a couple of times as the four of us hiked from our hotel wing through a warren of hallways, past the gift shop, lobby and nature area, until we arrived at the bar.

Paul, the insurance man, was apparently doing calculations in his head. When we were seated with our drinks, he said, "Construction costs on this place must have run well into the millions. It's a pretty amazing investment for rural West Michigan."

"I agree," said Frank, "and of course it's all borrowed money."

"Of course, but apparently the lenders had faith in the business plan."

"And so far it looks like they were right—in calculating that a lot of people were just waiting for a chance to gamble. From what I hear, the place is making money. The hotel wing we're staying in went up about a year ago."

"Some people get really addicted to gambling," said Jewell, "and others just manage it as entertainment. Fiona used to bring her mother up here about once a month."

"Does she still do that?" I wondered.

"I think so," she said. "There was a problem for a while when her mom went on continuous oxygen."

"I expect that oxygen would not be welcome in a place with so many people smoking."

"That's right," said Jewell. "But then she got an oxygen concentrator. The concentrator is not flammable, so now Fiona's mom can resume her gambling."

"Ah, the wonders of modern science."

At a quarter to seven we made our way to the Hawks Nest, which turned out to be a circular room with about thirty round tables arranged under a beamed ceiling. The four of us joined two couples already seated at one of the tables. There must have been over a hundred people in the audience and the demographic was middle-aged and older. Formally clad waiters circulated throughout the room, providing baskets of breadsticks and pouring coffee for everyone.

"I'd love some real food," Paul said as he grabbed a breadstick.

"Me too," I said. "Frank offered to stop in Manistee but I was saving my appetite."

The next waiter who approached gave us each a program that announced, "Tony and Tina's Wedding." Apparently we were cast as the wedding guests.

What followed over the next ninety minutes was a dozen actors presenting every wedding cliché ever imagined, including the pregnant bride, the jilted lover, the angry in-laws and a bunch of other stuff that I'm sure I missed because I was hungry and increasingly angry that the dinner part of the dinner theatre was not forthcoming.

I drank more coffee and even added sugar in an attempt to raise my blood sugar and my spirits. But the caffeine only made me jumpy. It took a lot of effort on my part not to complain because, after all, we were supposed to be having a good time.

It was closing in on nine o'clock when the unhappy couple departed on their honeymoon. And we, the wedding guests, were finally turned loose at the buffet table. The offering was predictable—lasagna, salad and green beans with the nice addition of Alaskan salmon on wild rice. The wedding cake was pretty good if you like that gooey white frosting.

With food in my belly, my mood improved considerably. When Frank and Paul decided to go play poker, Jewell and I told them we were going to check out the pool and hot tub. As it turned out, we spent the rest of the evening there. Toward the end we were the only customers.

"This is wonderful," said Jewell, sliding down until the water came up to her neck. "Thanks so much for inviting us."

"Thanks for coming," I said. "It's not often that you and I get to spend this much time together."

"I wonder how much money our guys are losing."

"I wonder what's happening back in town."

"After work Monday," she said, "I can likely give you a full report on the beach party."

"A full report?"

"An eyewitness account."

"Okay, tell me. Who is your spy?"

"Fiona. She said she was going to be there."

"By herself?"

"On a date. Remember Joel, the lawyer friend?"

"Oh right."

"Well, it turns out that Ivy had invited him too. So Joel and Fiona are going together. She said it's their first real date."

"How nice. I hope it goes well for them."

"Me too. She hasn't had the greatest luck with men."

It was after eleven when a uniformed woman appeared and told us that the pool area was closing and she had to lock up. Jewell and I decided we were so relaxed that all we wanted was to head for bed. We walked back to our rooms and said good night. I crawled into bed with a book but must have dozed off because the next thing I knew Frank was crawling in next to me. He might have said something, but I'm not sure what it was because I dropped off to sleep again.

But my sleep didn't last.

Some time around four in the morning, my excess coffee consumption kicked in, leaving me wide awake with Frank snoring peacefully next to me. I got up and used the bathroom, drank some water and lay down again. Half an hour later, I was still fully awake. I got up and sat in a chair where I tried to read a book by the light of a desk lamp. But I couldn't concentrate. I stood and looked out the window. A half moon was near the horizon and I heard a mournful cry come floating out of the woods. I figured it was an owl—or maybe a loon.

I was ready to try for bed again when something caught my attention. A white van was pulling into the empty parking lot. Curious, I stayed at the window and watched. The driver of the van got out, opened a side door and removed a container which he carried into the building. It looked like a picnic cooler. Why was he making a delivery at four in the morning?

Minutes later, the driver returned with another man and they each carried another container into the building. Then the guy came out alone, started up the engine and drove away. I turned out my light and crawled into bed next to Frank. It must have been close to six when I finally drifted off to sleep.

CHAPTER TWENTY-ONE

"Tracy, wake up." Frank was shaking my shoulder, none too gently.

"What for?" To my befuddled mind, there was nothing on earth more desirable than another hour of sleep.

"We promised to meet Paul and Jewell for the breakfast buffet."

"Oh, that." I opened my eyes. "What time is it?"

"Twenty of nine."

"Oh crap, why didn't you wake me?"

"Believe me, I tried. You mumbled a few words so I figured you were awake and I went to take a shower. And now you're—well, you're seriously behind schedule."

"Okay, okay—sorry." I crawled out, found my clothes and proceeded to get dressed. "Guess I don't need a shower," I said. "I had plenty of tub time last night." In the bathroom, I gave minimum attention to my hair and face. I was barely presentable when Paul and Jewell arrived.

Since no one had taken advantage of the in-room coffee, there was little in the way of conversation as the four of us made our way to the breakfast room. We let Frank do the navigating.

"Oh look," Jewell said as we took a final turn and entered a large, airy room where morning light spilled in through tall windows.

"And look at this," I said making a bee line for the coffee counter where I snagged a mug and filled it. I inhaled deeply and felt invigorated by the scent of almond mocha.

We joined a line of guests and focused on making the best possible selection from the ample buffet. When I tucked into my waffles, eggs, sausage, and blueberry muffin with marmalade, I began to feel human again. The coffee woke up some brain cells and that's when I remembered the peculiar delivery I had observed in the early morning hours. I wanted to tell Frank about it, but he and Paul were in a deep discussion about fly fishing versus deep water fishing. I decided to save the story for later.

After breakfast, I felt a hundred percent better. The men went to see if the roulette table was open, so Jewell and I decided to try our luck at the slot machines. An hour later, I was even and Jewell was two dollars ahead. We held a short conference and decided that neither of us wanted to spend any more time in that world of flashing lights and high pitched noises.

So we walked out to the lobby where the natural light was a relief all by itself. We checked out the announcements of coming events which leaned toward country singers and psychics. Then we sat for a while in the nature area, lulled by the soothing sound of falling water.

"Let's try the gift shop," said Jewell.

"Okay with me. Maybe they have baby clothes."

The gift shop didn't have any baby clothes, but it did have a lot of stuff—and most of it was expensive. There were beaded necklaces and earrings, tooled leather belts and wallets, oil paintings, woven rugs and stone carvings. We were admiring a display of feathered items called dream catchers when Jewell's phone rang.

"I'd better take this," she said.

Jewell stepped out of the store area with the phone in her hand. By the time she returned I was making a purchase.

"I didn't lose anything gambling," I said. "I figured I should drop a little money here."

"Fair enough," she said. Then her face turned serious. "I really hate to break up the party, but that was Sarah. She and Mark are up north at his folks' place and they would like to stop and see us this afternoon. "

"Don't apologize," I said. "We've had a great time and I wouldn't expect you to pass up a chance to see little Samantha."

"What did you buy?" Jewell said as we headed back to our rooms.

In reply, I opened a little gift box and showed her the contents—a stone turtle about two inches long. "It's a Petoskey stone," I said. "So it comes with its own turtle markings."

I dropped my purchase into my purse just as Frank and Paul caught up with us.

Jewell told Paul about the call from Sarah and said she thought they should head for home.

"Whatever you want," he replied. "How are we doing for time?"

"I had us almost packed before we went to breakfast," she said. "Hopefully we can be under way by noon."

So the four of us said our goodbyes in the hallway.

When Frank and I were alone in our room, we stretched out on the bed.

"Guess I didn't tell you," he said, "but I got Mardeen on the phone last night."

"What did he say? Is he willing to talk with you?"

"Yes. He agreed to me with me at,"—he looked at his watch—"at twelve-thirty. Possibly his lunch hour."

"And where are you meeting?"

"He gave me directions to the security manager's office. It's in another building."

"Which is probably half a mile from here."

"You're right. And it'll probably take me half an hour to find it. Too bad." He kissed me on the cheek, got up and went into the bathroom to check his appearance. "Sorry I have to leave," he said. "You going to be okay?"

"I'm fine. Think I'll take a little nap."

I must have fallen asleep within minutes. In any case, I had no idea what time it was when I became aware of someone opening the door. The someone turned out to be a short, dark skinned woman in a blue uniform. When I looked up and she registered my presence, the woman stammered an apology in slightly accented English.

"Oh miss, so sorry to disturb you. The other couple checked out so I think—I thought you were gone too. I come back later. So sorry."

"That's okay," I said. "I wasn't really asleep."

"Sorry," she said again as she turned to go.

"Hey," I said. "Can I ask you a question?"

She stood by the door with a pleasant but quizzical look on her face before she finally answered, "Sure. Okay." Clearly it was not often that hotel guests pursued conversations with the chamber maid.

I swung my feet around so I was sitting on the edge of the bed. This also gave me time to phrase my question. What came out was only a little bit of a lie. "I was hoping I might see a friend of mine up here. Her name is Lenore Cooper. Did you ever work with her?"

"Lenore? Sure, I work with her. She was my boss and a very nice boss. I was sorry when she left."

"What happened? Did she leave the area?"

"I don't know why she quit—but she don't go away. I saw her afterward at the K Mart. She tell me she got a job at a restaurant in town."

"In Manistee?"

"Yes. Manistee."

"Do you know which restaurant?"

"That nice place on the river. Some number West."

"880 West?"

"That's it. I see it but I never eat there. Cost too much."

"I've never been there either but I've heard about it."

"She say it is a much nicer job, even though it don't pay as good."

"Is that the place with deep fried ice cream?"

She smiled. "Yes, she tell me that is their specialty." We both laughed about the challenge of making that particular dessert. "I have to keep working," she said.

"Of course. I'm sorry to take your time."

"I don't mind," she said. "Not many people want to talk. If you see Lenore, tell her hello from Cecilia."

I thanked Cecilia for her help and she left. Then I took another stab at reading my book, and managed about ten pages before Frank returned.

"Sorry I took so long," he said. "Looks like it's nearly check out time."

"That's okay," I said. "We don't have much to pack."

Frank gathered up a few items from the bathroom and tossed them into my bag. "Did you find Mardeen?" I said.

"Yep."

"Any news?"

"A little. I'll tell you later."

"And I've got some news for you too."

He looked at me askance. "You picked up news during your nap?"

"You might say that."

We did a quick sweep of the room to make sure we were not leaving anything behind. We both picked up our jackets, I got my purse and he grabbed the overnight case. As we were leaving the room, Frank looked wistfully at the bed.

"We never did get around to testing that mattress."

CHAPTER TWENTY-TWO

"Did you say deep fried ice cream?"

"Yes, I did. I'd like to stop in Manistee for some deep fried ice cream."

"Never heard of it. You're not hallucinating, are you?"

Frank and I were in the casino parking lot trying to locate his vehicle. The sun was high and the heat was radiating off the pavement.

"Believe me, that place is enough to cause hallucinations—but no, I'm not making this up." We found the Blazer and he opened it. When I climbed inside, a blast of hot air enveloped me and the seat covers burned my legs. "It feels like an oven in here. Can you put on the air conditioning?"

"Sorry, the AC isn't working. Just put the window down and you'll feel better soon."

"I hope so. I can hardly breathe."

"Didn't you say you were tired of winter?"

"Yes, but I'm still not ready for this."

"Welcome to Michigan."

Frank drove to the edge of the parking lot and stopped in the shade of a maple tree. We opened both of our doors, hoping that the hint of spring breeze might help to cool things down.

"Before we go any where," he said, "let's compare notes. What brought on this yearning for deep fried ice cream?"

"Oh, that. Sure." I picked up a piece of cardboard and tried to use it as a fan. "Here's what happened while you were gone. The maid came in to make up our room. Because Paul and Jewell had checked out, she thought that we were gone too. When she saw me, she apologized and started to leave. Before she got away I asked if she knew anyone named Lenore Cooper. Turned out that she did. The maid, her name was Cecilia, told me that Lenore used to be her boss but, sometime after the holidays, Lenore quit and moved on. She landed a new job at a restaurant in town—a place called 880 West."

"Do you know this restaurant?"

"I've never actually been there. But they are famous for their desserts, especially the—."

"The deep fried ice cream. I get it."

"Right—so it seemed like this might be the perfect opportunity to, well, combine business with pleasure." I threw down my makeshift fan, which didn't seem to be having any effect. "But maybe none of this is important. Maybe Mardeen told you something that busted this case wide open."

Frank shook his head.

"Did Mardeen stand you up?"

"No, he kept the appointment."

"So what happened?"

"I met Lyle Mardeen in his office and he gave me a cup of yesterday's coffee. When I showed him the victim sketch, he said he had seen the woman coming into the casino."

"How could he be so sure it was her?"

"Said he got a good look at her because she came up and asked him for directions to Cooper's office. I asked him if he could place the time of year. He said as near as he could recall it was early October."

"I guess that computes. Did he see her when she left?"

Frank shook his head. "Mardeen said he went off shift then so he wasn't around when she left."

"Too bad. It would help to know what she was driving—if she was driving."

"So then I asked if there was anything else he could remember about her—how tall, her build, how she was dressed, how she talked, her walk, general mannerisms."

"What did he remember?"

"A lot of what he said wasn't exactly helpful," Frank said with a shrug.

"Average height and weight. Normal dress for the time of year—meaning jeans or slacks and a jacket—possibly a denim jacket. Nothing unusual about her speech, although he did say he got the feeling that she wasn't exactly a local."

"What made him think that?"

"At first he said she was dark-skinned but it could have been just a suntan. And of course, we have both Mexicans and Indians in the area. But he thought her face showed a lot of sun exposure. More than anyone would have in Michigan in October."

"So we're talking about the South or Southwest. Did she have dark straight hair?"

"He thought so. Certainly wasn't a blonde. Then I asked if he remembered if she was wearing any jewelry."

"Did he?"

"Yes, he said she wore what the Indians call a medicine bag. It was hanging around her neck on a leather strip."

"Sounds like she's our victim," I said, wondering once more if that leather thong had been the murder weapon. "Anything else?"

"Well, you were right in guessing that he doesn't think too highly of his boss, Marvin Greenwater."

"Everyone loves to complain about the boss. Even me. Did Mardeen have anything specific to offer?"

"Yes. He said it was no secret among the female staff that Greenwater engaged in what we would call sexual harassment. Sometimes it was inappropriate remarks. Other times it was physical contact."

"Did anyone ever try to report him?"

"Sounds like there was no one above him for them to talk to. Anyone who complained was out of a job."

"Maybe that's why Lenore Cooper doesn't work here any more."

"We'll probably figure that out when we see her," said Frank. "Are you sure this restaurant is open on Sunday?"

"They'd be foolish to close," I said. "The place is right on the river and I'm sure that tourism is a big part of their business."

"Then let's hope that Cooper is working today. Are you ready to go?"

"I'm ready."

We closed the doors of the Blazer, which had now cooled down to a bearable temperature, then buckled up and headed to Manistee.

"Oh hell," Frank said minutes later when a pair of flashing red lights appeared ahead of us. The road was blocked by a black and yellow wooden barrier. He hit the brakes and slowed to a stop.

"Hey, I don't mind," I said. "I've never seen this before."

"Miracles and wonders."

We had a front row seat as the bridge in front of us split in two and the half that we could see rose up before our eyes.

"This is great," I said as a pair of sailboats with bare masts started to motor downriver toward the bridge "It reminds me of *Danger at the Drawbridge.*"

"What was that—a Hitchcock movie?"

"No, it was a book. I guess you never read the Nancy Drew mystery stories."

"Never heard of them."

"They were kid books. I guess today you'd call them young adult novels."

"Didn't read much when I was young. Except comic books. I had a box of them under my bed that I traded with other kids. Just ask me anything about Tarzan or Superman."

"And probably Wonder Woman too."

"Sure, all the boys loved Wonder Woman."

The boats had now cleared the bridge, but the red lights continued to flash and the guard rail didn't budge.

"What do you read now?" I said.

"I like books by Lee Child."

"Never heard of him. What are his books about?"

"A guy named Jack Reacher. He's sort of a modern day Lone Ranger—a drifter who meets people in trouble and helps them. And along the way he always has to beat the holy crap out of somebody."

"I'll have to check him out."

"I think you would like him."

The boats had slipped away down the river and the bridge was eased back down. Finally the red lights went off and the gates lifted. We drove onto the bridge.

"I think as soon as we cross you should look for a right turn," I said.

"Okay. But how well do you know this town?"

"I'm just guessing. But the place we're going is on the river."

"Good thinking."

"And then, if we're not on West Street, we should try to find it."

"And your reasoning is?"

"Because the name of the restaurant is also the address."

"Oh, clever. 880 West. And you know all this because—."

"Because they advertise with us sometimes—well, at least twice a year."

My directions were good and a few minutes later Frank scored a parking place in front of an art gallery in the seven hundred block of West Street. We had no trouble finding the restaurant. It was overlooking the river, a black one-story building with grey trim, neat but not showy.

We stepped inside and found ourselves in a busy dining area that was bustling with the lunch time crowd, with quite a few tables occupied by families. A sign suggested that we wait to be seated. So we waited, but not very long. We were soon approached by a thirty-something woman wearing high heels and a grey dress that draped nicely on her figure.

"The indoor seating is filled," she said. "Would you mind being seated on the deck?"

"Outdoor seating would be fine," said Frank.

"As long as it's not in the sun," I added.

"Every table has an umbrella," she assured us.

We followed the woman out onto the deck, where she put us at a table overlooking the river and adjusted the umbrella. There was only one other party on the deck. As the hostess handed us menus, I looked her over, hoping to spot a name tag, but there was none. On closer examination, I decided that she was in her forties but wearing her age very well.

"One of our servers will be with you shortly," she said as she turned to leave.

"Oh, just a minute—I have a question," I blurted. Frank and I hadn't discussed how we were going to play this, but I made a quick decision not to wait. The woman stopped and looked at me, clearly impatient, with half an eye on the newest arrivals waiting in the foyer.

"I'm trying to find Lenore Cooper," I said, keeping my voice low. "I understand she works here."

The woman maintained a professional smile but her eyes registered mild alarm at my question. "I'm Lenore Cooper," she said with another glance at the foyer. "But as you can see, I'm very busy. What is it you want?"

I kept hoping Frank would help me out, but he was silent. "We just want to ask you a couple of questions," I said. "Will you have any time—later on today?"

Her smile disappeared. "Are you from the casino? Did Marvin send you?"

"No no, I promise, this has nothing to do with—with your old boss." I directed a beseeching look at Frank.

"Please don't be alarmed," he said. "I'm a detective from Cedar County. I'm hoping you can help us with a missing person case."

Now Cooper looked hesitant—as though she was trying to decide whether or not to believe us. She glanced again at the foyer. Finally she said, "I get off at two-thirty. I usually stop at that bookstore across the street. Look for me there."

And with that she was gone.

"I hope you didn't mind," I said to Frank as we picked up our menus. "I just got the feeling that she would respond better if the opening came from a female."

"You took me by surprise," he said, "but I think you were right. She probably wasn't going to come back to our table again. So it was our best chance to approach her without being conspicuous."

"The question about her old boss suggests that you may have been right about some—ah—friction between the two of them." I opened my menu, but then laid it down again. "Tell me," I said, "why do you still refer to our victim as a missing person?"

"Think about it. Our question was intrusive enough. How do you think she would react to someone wanting to talk about a murder?"

"Not very well, I guess." I retrieved the menu and started to review the offerings. "Since this is actually my lunch, I guess I'd better eat a salad before I have my deep fried ice cream."

"Do they have it?"

"Of course," I said. "It's right there on the bottom of page four."

CHAPTER TWENTY-THREE

After lunch, Frank and I walked across the street to the bookstore Lenore Cooper had mentioned. It was called the Book Nook. The place was quiet, with most of the customers hidden among the long aisles of books. Looking around, I spotted a reading area by the front window where comfy chairs surrounded a low coffee table that was covered with disarranged newspapers.

"Let's wait here," I said. We can watch the front door."

"I wonder if she'll even show," said Frank as he lowered himself into one of the chairs.

"I think she will. In any case, it's a nice place to wait." I took a chair and picked up a flyer that featured a copy of the current best seller list. "Smells like they have a coffee bar here."

"Maybe she just sent us over here so she could get away from us." Frank was staring at the front door, ignoring the coffee aroma as well as the reading material.

"Maybe she did. But do you have any better ideas on how to get her to talk to us?"

"I can usually think of something."

"It's not like you can threaten to take her in for questioning."

"That's not what I had in mind."

"Cripes Frank, relax. We're not even in your jurisdiction."

I was trying to figure out what had put Frank in such a negative mood when the question became irrelevant—because the front door opened and Lenore Cooper walked in. She walked past us to the opposite side of the store and spoke briefly to the young black man behind the counter. Minutes later, he handed her a frothy looking coffee drink in a heavy white mug. She held the cup while she turned around to survey the store.

It didn't take her long to spot Frank and me.

I gave her a little wave and debated on whether to stand up. I felt like we were trying to approach some wild animal that might bolt if we were too forward. She met my eyes but didn't move for a few minute. I held my breath.

Frank was watching her too with an intense look on his face.

"Don't scare her off," I whispered.

Taking my cue, Frank rearranged his features into some semblance of a smile. That's when Lenore Cooper took a sip of her coffee and began to walk in our direction. She stopped in front of us and said, "What is it you want from me?"

Suddenly Frank was all charm. He stood and offered his chair. "Please sit down," he said. "You've been on your feet for a while."

Cooper hesitated only a moment before sinking into the chair. She pulled off her shoes and sighed. "Damn heels," she said, "worst part of the job."

"I agree with you on that," I said. "Whoever invented those devices should be forced to walk in them—for eternity."

Frank sat in another chair and pulled it up close so we made up a cozy triangle. He pulled out his wallet and showed Cooper his identification. "I'm a detective," he said, "from Cedar County. We're hoping maybe you can give us some information."

"Not my stomping grounds," she said. "I haven't been to Cedar County in years."

"That's okay. We're hoping you can help us identify this woman." He produced a miniature version of the sketch we had been using earlier. "Do you remember ever meeting her?"

"Maybe. Let me take a closer look."

He handed it over. While she scrutinized the picture Frank said, "We think that while you were working at the casino she may have come in to apply for a job."

"You seem to know a lot about me."

"I apologize if all of this seems intrusive. But it's very important. Do you remember her?"

"Well, I see a lot of job applicants but, yes, I'm pretty sure that she was one of them."

"Do you remember her name?" said Frank.

"Oh come on, you're asking a lot." She rolled her eyes. "What I remember is that she made a pretty good impression. I thought she would be a good worker. So I gave her the application form. She took it and said she would come back in a few days if she wanted to follow through."

"Did she ever come back?"

"No. She never came back. So now—you said she's gone missing?"

"The fact is," said Frank, "she is dead."

"Oh." Cooper's hand jerked, nearly spilling her coffee. "What happened?"

"We don't know," he said. "We've been dealing with an unidentified body. So anything you can tell us would be helpful."

Lenore Cooper was silent, staring down at the table.

"Just take your time," said Frank. "Try to visualize the meeting, see what comes to mind."

Cooper closed her eyes and took a deep breath. After a few seconds she spoke. "Okay, her name was Diane or Deana or one of those D words. Maybe Delane. Yes it had an L in it. I'm sure she was new in town because she didn't have any local references. I think she was from Arizona or Oklahoma. That, along with her appearance, made me pretty sure she was part Indian."

By now Frank had his tiny notebook in hand and was scribbling in it. "Did she indicate why she had come to Michigan?"

"I got the feeling that she had some family here."

"Was she staying with a family member?"

"I don't know."

"Can you give us a last name? That would help a lot."

She shook her head. "Sorry, the last name escapes me. I saw an awful lot of applicants last fall—because we were opening a new wing on the hotel."

"Do you keep any kind of records? Did you write down her last name anywhere?"

"Nope. If she had brought the application back, I would have kept that on file for a year—but I never had one."

"Okay. Can you remember anything else—anything at all about your conversation with her?"

We were all silent for a moment. Then Cooper said, "It seems like she had a meeting scheduled in Ludington in a couple of days—something about a lawyer. Said she would know more after the meeting."

Frank looked up from his scribbling. "Did she mention the name of the lawyer?"

She shook her head again. "Sorry."

"That's okay. Anything else?"

She shook her head.

"Well, thanks for helping us out." Frank folded up the notebook, then slipped it into his pocket.

But Cooper wasn't ready to go. "My turn now," she said. "I have a couple of questions for you two."

"Sure."

"Who told you where I was working?"

"It was purely by chance," I said. "Frank and I were staying at the hotel. When Cecelia came in to make up the room, I asked her if she knew anything about you. She told me you were a very good boss but you had left the casino and found yourself a better job—in a restaurant."

"Okay. But how did you get my name?"

I looked at Frank. He nodded in my direction. "We got that from Lyle Mardeen," I said.

"And how did you find Lyle?"

"Lyle found us," said Frank. "We went to the casino and showed around the sketch. Eventually Lyle saw the picture. He contacted us and said he was pretty sure he had seen the woman last fall when she asked him for directions to your office."

Lenore Cooper was silent, a frown on her face.

"Did you have problems with Mardeen?" I said.

"Oh no, Lyle is okay. Marvin Greenwater is the one I can't stand."

"I hear the women don't like him much," I said.

"That is an understatement." Her words were accompanied by an unladylike snort. "But I won't say any more." She finished her coffee and put down the cup. "Are you through with me?"

"I believe we are," said Frank. "Do you have any more questions for us?"

"I guess not."

"In that case, thanks for your time and I hope we didn't alarm you." He pulled a card from his wallet. "Here's my phone number. In case you think of anything else about her—any detail, however tiny—don't hesitate to call."

Cooper slipped her feet back into her shoes. She took the card and put it in her purse. "I do have one more question."

"Go ahead," said Frank.

"You said Delane was dead. What happened to her?"

The silence was deafening. I glanced at Frank and he nodded to me. I shook my head. So he leaned close and spoke quietly to the woman we had been tracking. "She was murdered," he said.

Cooper sat motionless for few seconds. Then she nodded silently, stood and walked away from our little triangle. Abruptly she turned and came a few steps back toward us.

"If I was you," she said, "I'd take another look at Marvin Greenwater."

Frank's eyebrows shot up. "Any special reason—for suspecting Greenwater?"

"Just because he's an all around bastard," she hissed.

And with that she turned on her three-inch heel and walked out.

CHAPTER TWENTY-FOUR

The meeting with Lenore Cooper left Frank and me with a lot to think about—especially her comment about Marvin Greenwater. We sat in silence for a few minutes until I glanced around and saw the store clerk looking at us.

"After taking advantage of their space," I said, "I feel like we should buy something. Also because I'm about to look for their restroom."

"Sure. Want some coffee?"

"No, I had enough of that with lunch. I think I'll check out the mystery section."

So Frank and I spent some time browsing. When I found the shelf with mysteries by Michigan authors I picked out two books—one by Elizabeth Buzelli and another by Aaron Stander. Frank was happy to find the latest from Lee Child.

We were on our way home when I said, "What do you think about that comment from Cooper?"

"Which one?"

"That we consider Marvin Greenwater—as a suspect. I mean, that's what she was suggesting wasn't it?"

"I've been thinking about that. So far it's hard to see a strong connection. Unless he and the victim had a past that we know nothing about."

"Let's assume they did. He may have thought she had a reason for wanting a job at the casino."

"Possible. But what would it be?"

"Maybe work there a while and then blow the whistle for sexual harassment."

"All possible—but—."

"I know—sheer speculation."

"Speculate away," he said. "Since we don't really have any solid suspects."

"Guess we don't. But we do have a first name."

"That we do. And something about an appointment with a lawyer."

"Is there anything we can do with the lawyer angle?" I said.

"Not much."

"Couldn't you canvass all the lawyers in Ludington about a broken appointment with someone named Delane?"

"I don't think we'd get much. Client confidentiality and all that."

"Does that apply if the client is dead?"

"Debatable. But without an obituary, there's no proof that the woman is dead."

"Sort of a catch twenty-two. So much for that idea. We really haven't made much progress."

"I wouldn't say that. We know more than we did when we left town yesterday."

It was almost four o clock when we pulled into my driveway. Les was on his front porch painting a chair and Daisy was sweeping the steps. I waved at them as we walked up my driveway and Les waved back. When we reached my front door, Frank rather abruptly grabbed my hand and pulled me into the house.

"So you don't want to talk with our neighbors?" I said.

"Nothing against your neighbors—but I was thinking."

"About what?"

"I was thinking we should make up for lost time. The fact is that I took you away for a romantic night in a motel and we didn't even—."

"No, we didn't. We never found any time for hanky panky."

"So how about it?"

"I think it's a good idea."

We were heading for a clinch but then Frank—who always notices things—pointed out the frantically blinking light on my message machine.

"Maybe you should check that out," he said.

"Okay. Let's hope it's not Marge." I pressed the red button. There were three messages in all.

The first was from a man who didn't bother to identify himself. The voice was gravelly, the recording punctuated with pauses, deep breaths and possible a sob. "Tracy," it said, "I need your help.—It sounds crazy, I know, but I'm—well, I'm in jail. In, ah, I guess I'm in Stanton. I just didn't know who else to call—. If you're there, please pick up." That was where the message ended.

"Who the hell was that?"

"I'm afraid that was the person I've been doing my damnedest to avoid."

"And who would that be?"

"That would be Steven—my ex-husband."

The next message was from Ivy Martin.

Ivy was wondering if I had any cash on hand to help get her boyfriend out of jail. "It was all a big mistake," she said. "And I am just furious with that deputy, Curt Laman. He's a big bully who just likes to push people around. Call me when you get this."

The third message was from Fiona. "Hi Tracy. Your ex made quite a hit at the party last night. Too bad you missed all the excitement. Call me."

"What the hell went on last night ?" I said, thinking it was a rhetorical question.

But Frank already had his cell phone out. "The sheriff ought to know," he said as he punched in a number. But Sheriff Benny didn't answer, so Frank called the jail. "Do you have a guy in there named Steven Quinn?"

I moved closer to Frank so I could hear the reply. "I just came on," said a female voice, "so let me check.—Okay, we did have a person by that name. We kept him overnight but someone bailed him out this morning."

"And what was he in for?"

"The charges were—let's see, these guys have terrible handwriting—it looks like disturbing the peace, drunk and disorderly, assault and, oh yes, resisting arrest."

By now I had started to giggle at the pictures my mind was conjuring. I just couldn't help myself.

Frank smiled as he ended the call. "Looks like you dumped a real loser."

"He never got arrested when I was with him."

Frank put an arm around me. "So tell me," he said. "Does this news call for any action on your part?"

"Not a thing." I shook my head to emphasize my total disinterest in what might or might not be happening to Steven Quinn.

"Then maybe we can resume our interrupted trip to the bedroom."

"I'm definitely ready for some bedroom time," I said. "Just don't be disturbed if I burst out laughing at an inappropriate moment."

"I'll take it as a compliment."

Frank and I managed nearly an hour of intimacy and I was starting to doze off when the mood was interrupted by an insistent trilling sound that came from somewhere on the bedroom floor.

"What the heck?"

"It's my phone."

Apparently Frank's cell phone was in the pocket of his pants which had been hastily discarded on the floor during our rush to passion. "Sorry," he said, as he disentangled himself. "I'd better take that."

He retrieved the phone and answered it while sitting on the edge of my bed. "Kolowsky here," he said.

To me he whispered, "It's Sheriff Benny."

"Yeah," he said to Benny, "I was just wondering what all the fracas was last night on the beach. What did that guy do to get everyone so upset?"

Despite my best efforts at eavesdropping, I couldn't pick up much of the sheriff's reply which went on for a few minute. But I was pretty sure that I caught the name Clint Pomeroy.

"Okay, give," I said as soon as Frank had ended the call.

Frank deposited the phone on my beside table and stretched out again before he replied. "Ivy rented a cottage for the beach party."

"We knew that. We were invited."

"I guess the cottage was in what you would call an inauspicious location. It was next door to Clint Pomeroy's summer place."

"I thought he never went there."

"He was there last night."

"Maybe he wanted a quiet weekend."

"If so, he didn't get it. He decided that Ivy's party was too loud so he went over and asked them to tone it down. Didn't help much so he went back a second time. I guess your ex—."

"Don't call him that."

"I guess what's-his-name—."

"Steven."

"I guess on the second visit, Steven got belligerent with Pomeroy. They exchanged insults and threats. One of them threw a punch. The neighbors on the other side were watching and they're the ones who called the cops. The village police responded and Curt Laman was on boat patrol so he came over too. Pomeroy got quiet right away. But that Quinn guy just kept arguing and blustering and finally called them a bunch of small town dumb fucks. That's when Laman put the cuffs on him."

"What a story. I don't know whether to laugh or cry."

"Aren't you glad we were out of town?"

"I am. But now I wish I had changed my name. This is going to show up in the paper."

"Just pretend you never heard of him."

"I'll do my best."

Frank and I got dressed and took a walk downtown where we checked out boats in the village marina. He talked with a couple of charter boat captains about fishing conditions. When we arrived back home, we were feeling more sociable so we stopped to visit with Les and Daisy who insisted on giving us iced tea and ginger cookies. To my considerable relief, they hadn't heard anything about the ruckus on the beach so we didn't have to do any explaining. The conversation centered mainly around raising vegetables and how to protect them from rabbits.

Back at the house, Frank helped me dig up a patch of ground where I wanted to plant some greens. By the time we finished, were hungry enough to raid the refrigerator and put together sandwiches for supper. It was about nine o'clock when he left.

As soon as he was gone, I lost no time in calling Jewell. But her line was busy.

Then I remembered that Fiona had invited me to call her. So I did.

"Hey Fiona," I said, "tell me about Saturday night—the party at the lake."

"Oh, it was a kicker," she said. "I think I told you I was going with Joel Dukes."

"He's that nice looking lawyer—?"

"Yep. This was sort of our first date."

"Sounds like you won't forget it soon. So how many people were at the party? Was it really all that noisy? And what in blazes went on?"

"Let's see. There were maybe a dozen people when we arrived—and more kept showing up. A lot of beer but also some of the hard stuff. Things were going okay as long as we stayed in the house. But then it was time to build a bonfire and roast hot dogs and somebody passed out jello shots and somebody else lit some firecrackers. So this guy, this Clint somebody, comes over and says could we keep the noise down."

"That was Clint Pomeroy. He owns—or he did own the Pomeroy Inn."

"The place that burned down?"

"Yes, that one."

"Well, no wonder he was in a bad mood."

"I think he's always in a bad mood."

"Maybe so. Anyway, Ivy seemed to know him so she went over and flirted with him a little—no, make that a lot—and asked him to join the party. He said he didn't give a damn about the party and he was trying to get some sleep. So he and Ivy talked some more and then he went back to his place."

"Did the party quiet down?"

"Not for long. It was maybe half an hour later when Joel and I were getting ready to leave that Pomeroy shows up again, this time not so polite. This time Ivy wasn't polite either. She said he'd been making plenty of noise all day with his damn motorcycle so she could have a party if she wanted to."

"Wait a minute—Pomeroy has a motorcycle?"

"Seems he does."

I pictured the businessman I had interviewed. "He doesn't seem the motorcycle type."

"Probably his midlife crisis. All these buttoned-down types want to play Easy Rider on the weekends."

"So then what?"

"So now Ivy isn't being polite any more. She's mouthing off about his motorcycle. And he's giving it back to her. So then, your Steven Quinn—"

"Please don't call him mine."

"Oops, sorry. So Ivy's new boyfriend steps up beside her and starts yelling insults at Pomeroy. Things in general are pretty tense. The rest of us are just standing there watching."

"Did they actually fight?"

"They got started. First it was a push, a shove back and then one of them, maybe Steven, took a swing at Pomeroy. And he swung back. They both went down and were rolling around in the sand. Fortunately, that's when the cops showed up."

"But Steven was the only one they took to jail?"

"Right. Well, of course, Pomeroy is a local plus he was sober and he immediately became very conciliatory with the cops—called them by name and everything. But Steven—he was on a roll and just couldn't seem to control himself. So finally—they took him away."

"What did Ivy do?"

"Ivy burst into tears and the party pretty much wound down from there."

"I understand he's out now."

"Yes, Ivy managed to borrow some money for bail."

"I wonder where she got it."

"She called everyone she knew——."

"Yes, she even called me."

"When she finally got around to Joel, he said yes, but he would deal with it in the morning. So Steven had to spend the night in the clink and Ivy took him home with her this morning."

"Joel sounds like a pretty decent guy."

"Yes, considering that he didn't know Steven Quinn at all. And he hardly knows Ivy."

I wondered for a moment if I should warn Fiona that Ivy had a habit of stealing boyfriends. But then I decided that Fiona was more than capable of protecting her own interests. After we said good night, I ran myself a hot bath. I figured that a good soak would relax me so I could fall asleep.

But the bath didn't work the way it was supposed to.

After I got to bed my body was relaxed but my brain stayed wide awake, reviewing everything that had taken place in the past two days. First there was the trip to the casino, then our meeting with Lenore Cooper and finally the unfolding news about Steven and the party. That's when I remembered something I had been meaning to tell Frank.

In all the excitement, I had forgotten to mention the white van that I saw in the casino parking lot making a delivery at four in the morning.

I made a mental note to tell Frank about it the very next time I saw him.

CHAPTER TWENTY-FIVE

"I hear your ex-husband got busted Saturday night."

It was Monday afternoon and I was working on a story about the village wastewater plant when Jake came by. His comment not only interrupted my train of thought, it also made me furious.

"And you're busy spreading the news all over town," I snapped.

"Hey, no offense." He turned and headed for his office.

I got up and followed him. "I thought you were my friend," I said.

"I believe I am, Tracy."

"Then how about trying for a little sensitivity in this area?"

"I'm sorry. I didn't think—I mean, it's been years hasn't it?"

"Jake, have you ever been divorced?"

"Well sure, once—actually twice, if you count the annulment."

"So think about it. Would it be fair to hold you responsible for everything your former wives have done since you parted company with them?"

"Lord no. One of them—well never mind what she did. Point taken.

I promise I won't mention the guy again—unless—."

"Unless what?"

"Oh—unless he kills someone."

"Not funny, Jake."

I went back to work but had trouble focusing on the graphs and statistics submitted by the village engineering firm. It took me the rest of the afternoon to put together a story and, even then, I knew it needed more work. The only good thing about the day was that Marge wasn't there.

I left the office in a dark mood which didn't improve until I got home and answered the phone to hear Jewell's voice.

"I'm on my way home from work," she said. "Okay if I stop by?"

"More than okay. It might be just what I need."

"I'll be there in a few minutes."

"Great. I'll put on the coffee."

Half an hour later, the two of us were ensconced on my living room sofa with cups of coffee and a plate of ginger cookies. Jewell showed me the latest pictures of her grandbaby and shared the news that Sarah and Mark had changed their wedding date to September. It had something to do with a job offer Mark had received from a firm in Toledo, Ohio.

"And, of course, you and Frank are invited to the wedding."

"Gosh, that will make two in one year. The last wedding we celebrated was Les and Daisy's."

"How are those two doing?"

"Frank and I talked with them yesterday. They're busy planting things and seem happy as a pair of clams." So far I had been avoiding any mention of Ivy's party but finally I said, "Jewell did you happen to talk with Fiona today at work?"

"I saw her at lunch but we hardly had time to talk. I asked her about Saturday night and she said it was a long story best shared in private."

"That's putting it mildly—and I'm relieved that the whole thing didn't get broadcast throughout the hospital cafeteria."

"So what is the news? Have you talked with her?"

"Yep, got a full report of the Saturday night disaster."

"So now I am curious." Jewell picked up a cookie. "What on earth went on at the beach party?"

So I relayed everything I knew to Jewell. I told her how Ivy's rental cottage just happened to be next to Clint Pomeroy's place. That Pomeroy came over to complain about the noise, twice, and the second time Steven got so belligerent that the cops were called and Steven spent the night in jail.

"On Sunday morning, Joel Dukes helped Ivy bail him out," I said, concluding the sad tale.

"What a fiasco," she said, stifling laughter. "Aren't you glad we weren't there?"

"Yes, and I'm glad I wasn't even home. I had messages on my machine from both Steven and Ivy."

"What did they want?"

"They wanted me to help."

"Would you have? I mean, if you'd been home, would you have done anything?"

"I'm not sure what I would have done. But since I wasn't even here, I didn't have to make that decision."

Jewell laughed. "Just think about it. Probably the altercation was going on just as you and I were relaxing in the hot tub."

I laughed too. But then I said, "Jewell, I certainly don't mind rehashing the incident with you. But I do feel uncomfortable with everybody in general knowing that this guy who came to town, started a fight, and got thrown in jail was my ex-husband."

"Of course you don't want it broadcast all over town—or all over the hospital. Fiona understood that."

"Yes, Fiona has a pretty acute sensitivity to situations like that."

"Probably because she had to endure so much gossip when her husband died last year."

"Looks like she has come through that pretty well," I said.

"Yes, Fiona tends to land on her feet."

"More coffee?" I offered.

"Thanks," she said, "but I'd better be on my way. But I also wanted to remind you about Thursday night."

"Thursday? Do we have something going on?"

"Indeed we do. That wine tasting event at the yacht club."

"I had almost forgotten. But sure, I'll go."

"Might as well," she said, "you already bought a ticket."

"And come to think of it, the ticket wasn't exactly cheap. How could I forget? It's some kind of benefit isn't it?"

"I think it's for the Humane Society."

"As long as they don't make me bring home a dog."

"Tracy, I think you need a dog."

"Maybe someday."

After Jewell had gone I noticed a message on my answering machine. I punched the button and heard Ivy's voice. "Tracy, call me just as soon as you get this. We need to talk. It's about Steven."

I started to punch in her number and then stopped, my finger in midair. Because I didn't want to talk to her about Steven. I didn't want to talk to Ivy about anything at all. Instead I decided to call Frank. But my call went to voice mail and I waited the rest of the evening, with growing impatience, for him to return the call

Jewell's visit had cheered me up, but now I was starting to feel moody again. I tried to sort out my thoughts and feelings. Among other things, it bothered me that I'd never had the chance to tell Frank about the white van I had seen that night at the casino. Sometimes the memory felt so hazy that I wondered if I had dreamed the whole incident. And maybe it wasn't important anyway.

Wednesday rolled around, the day our weekly paper comes out, and I was not looking forward to reading about Steven Quinn. I tried to ignore the stack of papers when it arrived in our office around four in the afternoon. Then Frank called and asked if he could stop by to see me after work.

"Please do," I said. "But be warned. I may be in a bad mood."

"Did I do something wrong?"

"No, it's not you. It's—well, you'll find out."

"I'll be ready."

So I grabbed a copy of the Shagoni River News just as I was leaving work. Arriving home, I plunked down in the porch swing and opened up the paper. I was scanning the first section when Frank arrived.

"At least it's not on the front page," I said as he sat down beside me.

"It's good to see you too," he said.

Ignoring his sarcasm, I opened the paper and continued my search until I reached the police report on the bottom of page ten. There it was under Saturday's date and I read it aloud. "Shagoni River Police Dept, *11:30 p.m., Steven Quinn, age 47, drunk and disorderly.*"

"Is this what got you upset?"

"Three lines in the police report," I said. "I guess that's all he was worth."

"Were you hoping for more?"

"No. But I was afraid there might be—oh, I don't know what I was afraid of."

"Maybe you were hoping for a headline. Something like '*Local reporter's ex-husband arrested at drunken party*'".

I was finally able to laugh. "I guess that's what I was imagining—in my most paranoid flights of fancy."

"Well, now you know. Half the people in town won't even connect him with you."

"Do a lot of people read the police report?"

"More than you would expect. Hey, I was in a meeting Monday when you called. I'm sorry I didn't get back to you."

"It's not the first time. But you are forgiven."

"Thanks. But now—you said you had something you wanted to tell me."

"I know I said that—but right now I can't even remember what it was."

"Maybe you can't think on an empty stomach. How about we go out and get something to eat?"

"Food. What a great idea. Give me five minutes to get ready."

Frank was right—about the empty stomach affecting my memory. Less than an hour later we were at the Lakeside Café, where I had a glass of wine in hand and a plate of whitefish in front of me. That's when I remembered what had been haunting me ever since Saturday night.

"Okay," I said. "I finally remembered what I've been wanting to tell you."

"I'm all ears."

"Saturday night at the hotel—well, it was Sunday morning—you were asleep but I woke up sometime around four in the morning. All that coffee had kicked in and was keeping me awake. Anyway, I saw something going on in the parking lot."

"Unusual time for parking lot action."

"Exactly. I saw a white van pull in and stop. The driver got out. It looked like he opened the side door of the van and carried something into the building A few minutes later he came out and another guy was with him. Both of them carried similar boxes from the van into the building. Then the driver came out and drove away."

"You're right. Pretty strange. How big were these packages?"

"Like so." I held my hands in front of me about two feet apart. "Actually they looked a lot like picnic coolers. Those insulated containers people pack with food for picnics."

"Usually beer."

"Well yes. But beer coolers are usually smaller."

"Depends on how much beer."

"Okay, but what do you think?"

"I think you're right that it was a strange time for a delivery. My first thought would be drugs. Although that's a pretty large volume for anything like cocaine. I guess it would have to be bales of pot."

"Hah! After Greenwater gave us that big speech about how clean and law abiding the place was."

"He probably says that to everyone. Maybe there's a good reason for his little spiel."

"I see your point." I was quiet for a few seconds, thinking. "I wonder if Lyle Mardeen is involved in this somehow."

"Did the second guy look like Mardeen?"

"No. This guy was too short. They both were."

"Doesn't mean Mardeen wasn't involved," he said.

"True, but if he was involved—why would he go through all that trouble in order to talk with us?"

"Maybe Mardeen knew there was something fishy going on at the casino and he wanted us to find out about it."

"Maybe. But then why didn't he say so?" I took a swallow of wine. "Besides, that place is his livelihood. I can't see why he would want to shut it down."

"Unless it's to spite Greenwater," said Frank. "Maybe he thinks Lenore Cooper got a bad deal."

"Maybe he's in love with Lenore Cooper."

"I think we're getting carried away here."

"Right. Sheer speculation. But anyway, now you know what I saw."

We finished our food and ordered dessert—lemon pie for Frank and chocolate cake for me. Two coffees.

"Hey," I said as I forked up a bite of the cake, "do you want to go to an overpriced wine tasting tomorrow?"

"You make it sound inviting. Unfortunately, I'm busy."

"Likely story, but I don't blame you. I think tickets are sold out anyway."

"So you'll have to carry on without me. But I do have a great idea for Saturday—if you're free that is."

"I will be unless Marge decides to send me somewhere. It's my weekend to be at her beck and call. What did you have in mind?"

"The Cedar County Indian Powwow. It's at the campground north of town this year."

"Clever man. I bet you're planning to bring that sketch of Delane and see if anybody recognizes her."

"Seems like a good place to ask. Besides, it might be fun. I've never been to a powwow."

"I haven't either. And you know what? I think Marge was planning to have me cover it for the paper."

"So we've got a date?"

"We've got a date."

After dinner, Frank and I took a walk on the beach and stayed to watch the sunset.

I was glad we had finally talked with Mardeen and hoped that the guy was finished with stalking us. On the beach we met a couple from Detroit, and they invited us back to their campsite for a beer. Sharing their campfire and conversation, I felt more relaxed than I had in a long time. Like they say, ignorance is bliss.

CHAPTER TWENTY-SIX

The wine tasting was the next day and Jewell had promised to pick me up. I didn't want to drink on an empty stomach, I ate a peanut butter sandwich for supper, which left me with just enough time to change clothes. I put on a denim skirt with a white top and slid my feet into a pair of sandals. When Jewell arrived, I was waiting on the porch.

"Hey, you dressed up," she said as I slid into the seat next to her.

"Got inspired by the weather," I said. "I think this is the first time I've worn a skirt since October."

"Same for me."

The ride downtown took only a few minutes but gave me enough time to wonder if I should have shaved my legs. Too late now. We were still a block from the Yacht Club when I saw parked cars lining both sides of the street.

"Looks like a good turnout," said Jewell.

"Which makes parking a challenge. We could have just walked from my place."

"Never fear." She took a hard right turn and maneuvered into the last spot in the parking lot behind the drug store.

The walk to the Yacht Club was less than a block. Jewell and I entered the foyer where we surrendered our tickets and were given plastic glasses.

Once inside, we were greeted by the low level rumble of a dozen conversations going on at once. The place was full of people milling about, drinking and talking. In addition to the regular bar, there were two long tables set up with wine bottles, each of them tended by members of the Humane Society who wore little hats with doggie ears.

"I'm not sure how this works," I said. "Where do we start?"

"Just hang on to your glass," she said, "and stay with me."

I followed Jewell and we got in line at one of the tables. While we waited, Jewell surveyed the selections and, when her turn came, pointed to a bottle of red. The man behind the bar, someone I knew but couldn't place, poured a generous portion into her glass.

"Just pick out something that looks good," she whispered.

I looked over the offerings and finally pointed to a bottle of white. With our glasses filled, Jewell and I started to move away, trying very hard not to spill our drinks as we bumped elbows with the room full of guests.

Jewell seemed to have a destination in mind. She was maneuvering toward the far side of the room where a number of round tables were set with crackers and cheese. Our progress was slowed as we exchanged greetings and small talk with people along the way. One of them was Kyle, my co-worker, who was taking photos for the paper.

"Please don't put me in any of your pictures," I begged.

"I try to avoid that," he said.

Then Jewell turned and waved to someone who had just arrived. "There's Fiona," she said, "and I believe she's got Joel with her."

I turned to get a view of the entrance. It was easy to spot Fiona in her bright green dress. Joel, the lawyer who seemed on his way to becoming her boyfriend, was in casual business attire, looking all square-jawed and handsome.

"They make a nice looking couple," I said.

"I agree. She has good taste in men."

When Fiona saw us, she brought Joel over and introduced him. We spent a few minutes exchanging pleasantries and then Fiona said, "If you two can snag a table, maybe we can come and sit with you."

"That's a good idea," said Jewell. "Let's plan on it."

Joel and Fiona moved off toward the bar.

"Let's try for that one," Jewell said, indicating a corner table where two couples were getting ready to leave.

But before I could move on, I spotted Ivy Martin. She was wearing a short leather skirt and had a multicolored shawl draped around her shoulders. Ivy stood and surveyed the room.

"Look who just walked in," I said to Jewell.

When Jewell saw Ivy, she let out a groan. "I don't think I can handle this."

There wasn't much that Jewell couldn't handle. But I didn't blame her for wanting to avoid the woman who had seduced her husband. Ivy had seen us and was heading our way like a heat-seeking missile.

"You go claim that table," I said to Jewell. "I'll run interference."

I wasn't eager to talk with Ivy either—but it seemed the least I could do for my friend. So I let Jewell leave and stayed put while Ivy approached. But just before she reached me, Ivy brushed elbows with Joel Dukes. Immediately she threw her arms around him in a dramatic gesture that displayed all the colors of her shawl.

"Joel, I am so in your debt," she said, loud enough that people turned to look at them. "You saved my life Saturday night. I just didn't know who to ask—and then I thought of you. I just don't know how to thank you."

Fiona stood by with a bemused smile as her date was manhandled.

Joel, his cheeks reddening, grabbed Ivy's wrists in an attempt to free himself.

"I just—I hope everything gets straightened out," he said. "How is, ah, Steven doing?"

"Oh him. He's home sulking," said Ivy. Then she noticed me. "And you, Tracy, I really need to talk with you."

Joel looked relieved when Ivy let go of him and turned her attention to me.

"Come on, you," Ivy said as she grabbed my hand and pulled me toward a nearby alcove that held a nearly empty coat rack.

"Ivy," I said, "take it easy." But I couldn't put up much resistance for fear of spilling my wine.

"Why didn't you warn me?" she demanded.

"Warn you—about what?"

"About Steven—his violent tendencies."

I took a sip of wine, while I tried to follow her line of reasoning. *So now this whole thing was my fault?* "Ivy, when I was with him, he didn't have any violent tendencies. Never—neither toward me or anyone else."

"I don't believe you."

I wanted to say that maybe being with her had put him over the edge but I swallowed that remark. I tried for a neutral tone. "Remember, it's been nearly fifteen years since I lived with Steven. I don't know what goes on in that man's head."

"But you—you practically fixed us up!"

This comment pushed me beyond the mere irritation I had been feeling. This was Ivy at her worst—needy, dramatic and irrational. "That is utter nonsense and you know it. You asked me for his e-mail and I gave it to you. Period. End of story."

"Still you should have warned me—."

"Ivy, don't try to involve me. He's not my problem."

Ivy was silent as she searched her purse for a tissue—extracted one, wiped her eyes and blew her nose. It was the old pity ploy—and somehow it worked. I went into my female commiseration mode—a territory that felt better than anger.

"Oh Ivy," I said, "you do seem to have a problem with men."

"Yes, I do," she agreed with a sniff. "Horrible luck."

"But you always manage to find another one." I nodded toward the bar. "Go get yourself some wine. The winter white is very good." And with that I managed to slip away.

I joined Jewell at a table, where she was talking with the dentist Fred Meeker and his wife. She smiled when I sat down next to her.

"Thanks for doing that," she whispered. "I guess I'll have to deal with Ivy someday but I just didn't feel up to it tonight."

"Glad I could help—but I'm not sure we're in the clear yet."

"Meaning?"

"She came in alone. She might decide to come and sit with us."

"She might," said Jewell, with a glance at the bar area. "But then again, she might have found herself another man to latch on to."

"Already?"

Jewell nodded. "Take a look."

I turned my head to search the monochrome crowed until I spotted that rainbow shawl again. Ivy was head to head, talking with a man who had just come in. The man was Clint Pomeroy.

From where I sat, it looked as though Ivy was engaging Pomeroy in the mode she normally used with men—flattering and flirtatious.

"Oh this is rich," I said. "She's trying to charm the man who broke up her party."

"Looks to me like she's not having much luck," said Jewell.

"I guess it's a good thing she didn't bring Steven along."

Just then Joel and Fiona joined us and we gave up watching Ivy while Jewell introduced them to Fred and Joyce Meeker. I asked Meeker if he was planning to run for village council again and he said he was undecided. After that, we all talked about wine; white versus red, Michigan versus California, domestic versus imported.

Now that there were six of us at the table and minimal danger of Ivy joining us, the mood grew more relaxed. Joel left and returned with a bottle of wine which he proceeded to share with us.

"It's called ice wine," he said, "from the Leelanau peninsula. The grapes are left on the vine and only picked after there has been a light frost."

Fiona tried it and said, "It's very sweet."

"That's the effect of the frost," he said. "It concentrates the sugar."

The wine was indeed excellent, and went down very well. The entire table shared a wide ranging conversation, but nobody mentioned my ex-husband or the ill fated beach party. Eventually I excused myself to go in search of the ladies room. The room in question was at the end of a long hallway and, when I got there, I found both stalls full and three women waiting.

Needless to say, it was several minutes before I embarked on my return trip.

As I approached the coat rack, I noticed two men on the other side engaged in conversation. A closer look revealed that the men were Joel Dukes and Clint Pomeroy. I started to acknowledge them but stopped short when I realized they were involved in a private business conversation. So, instead, I just slowed down and slipped into my eavesdropping mode.

"—know I need the money," said Pomeroy, "so just give me my share."

"I'm sorry but that's not how it works," said Joel. "We can't distribute anything until all the heirs are found."

"Damnit, who knows how long that will take! Who knows where the hell she is—she could be dead f'r all we know." He seemed to be slurring his words.

"I've got someone working on it. It's just a matter of time."

"I don't have time," said Pomeroy. "What I'm tryin' to tell you—."

But Clint Pomeroy never finished the sentence.

His wine slowly spilled and he stared blankly at the empty glass while it slipped from his hand. Then he made a croaking sound and his head jerked forward—just before he slumped over and fell to the floor.

CHAPTER TWENTY-SEVEN

A general murmur of alarm moved through the crowd. With Clint Pomeroy crumpled on the floor at his feet, Joel Dukes took out his cell phone and called 911. Within minutes, the two nurses in the house got word of a man down.

Jewell and Fiona pushed their way through the crowd and knelt beside him.

"His breathing is okay," said Fiona as she loosened his tie and unbuttoned the top of his shirt.

"Pulse is rapid but strong enough," said Jewell who had her fingers on Pomeroy's wrist. "Please stand back so he gets enough air."

Jewell's remark was directed to the onlookers who were crowding around to get a better view of the disaster. I did my best to keep out of the way while I wondered what might have triggered Clint Pomeroy's collapse.

Minutes later one of the gawkers announced that an ambulance had arrived. The crowd parted to make way for two EMT's, one male and one female. They had a stretcher with them. The guy seemed to recognize Fiona and said, "Should we bring in the oxygen?"

"His color looks okay," said Fiona. "He should be all right until you get him on board."

So the four of them, the two ambulance attendants and the two nurses, knelt down and rolled Clint Pomeroy onto the stretcher. After they adjusted the height of the stretcher, Joel and I held the doors open while they made their exit. Jewell and Fiona went outside and had a short conference with the emergency personnel.

Then Pomeroy, still unconscious and strapped to the stretcher, was loaded into the ambulance. The female EMT hopped into the back and the guy closed the door. Seconds later, the ambulance jerked away from the curb and the siren started keening as the vehicle headed out.

"You were near him when he went down," Jewell said as we watched the ambulance leave. "Do you have any idea what brought it on?"

"No idea," I said. "He was standing there talking to Joel, and then he just crumpled up and fell over."

Inside, things were slowly returning to normal. The crowd of onlookers melted away as people returned to their cheese and crackers, drinks and conversation. Jewell, Fiona and I went back to our table. The Meekers were already there and Joel arrived a few minutes later.

"I'll be back in a minute," Fred Meeker said as he stood and headed toward the bar. "After all that, I think we deserve another bottle of wine. Especially our two nurses."

"I wonder what happened to Pomeroy," said Joyce. "I can't believe he was falling down drunk."

"I don't think so either," said Jewell.

I glanced at Joel and realized that I was the only person who had overheard the somewhat heated exchange between him and Clint Pomeroy. I wondered if Joel was going to say anything about their conversation.

But Joel Dukes was circumspect. "I understand Clint has been under a lot of stress lately," he said, "especially since the fire."

"I still wonder about the rumors of arson," said Joyce.

"I've heard him complain about how long the insurance company is taking with its investigation," I said.

"You know," said Joyce, "when I was over by the bar, I thought I saw him swallow a pill and wash it down with wine."

"Oh, lord," said Fiona. "I hope it wasn't heart medication."

"Is he on heart medication?" I wondered.

"We don't really know," Jewell said with a glance at Fiona. "I think he came in the E R about a year ago. But it turned out not to be anything serious."

Just then, Fred Meeker returned with a bottle of merlot and proceeded to pour everyone a sample. The conversation drifted away from Clint Pomeroy and his problems. I guessed that either Jewell or Fiona might know something more about the state of the man's health but were not eager to share information that was supposed to be confidential.

About half an hour later, Jewell and I decided it was time to leave and said our goodbyes. We were on our way to the door when Ivy appeared again, almost as though she had been waiting for me. I tried to slip away but she latched on to me again, this time grabbing my wrist.

Jewell saw that I was caught and said, "I'll just wait for you outside."

"I'll only be a minute."

Apparently Ivy had been drinking enough to come up with a bright idea. "Tracy, old pal, I really hate to do this—but I need a favor."

I had already refused to lend her money and Steven was out on bail, so I wondered what she wanted now. I couldn't think of a thing to say so I just stood there and waited for the bomb.

Which landed quickly enough. Ivy tugged on a strand of her hair, appearing for all the world like a middle school student imploring her best friend. "You see," she said, "the thing is—the, ah, situation between me and Steven has—well—it's deteriorated."

"Deteriorated?"

"Yes, to the point where it's really difficult having him around. So I was wondering—could you put him up at your place—for a little while?"

I stared at her in disbelief.

"Just a couple of days—I mean you've got a big house."

I finally found my voice. "The answer is no and no and no. He's all yours, Ivy. Deal with it."

I hurried out and found Jewell waiting for me. "You won't believe this," I said. "You absolutely won't believe what Ivy wanted from me."

"Did she get what she wanted?"

"No, she did not."

On Saturday, Frank came by to take me to the powwow. First we had lunch at my house—ham sandwiches with deli potato salad. While we ate, I told him about Clint Pomeroy's collapse at the wine tasting.

"Anyone know what brought it on?" said Frank

"Nothing definite. Although I did hear him talking with Joel Dukes—arguing you might say—and it was about money."

"Something must have set him off."

"Jewell called this morning," I said as I got up to pour coffee. "She said they kept Pomeroy overnight but released him the next day. So apparently it wasn't anything very serious."

"Maybe he just drank too much."

"Maybe he mixed the wine with some med that shouldn't be combined with alcohol."

"That would do it. Ready to go?"

"I'm ready."

We put the dishes in the sink and got ready for our first ever Indian powwow. When we walked out onto the porch, an intense, sweet scent surrounded us.

"What's that smell?" said Frank

"Hyacinth," I said, pointing to the clusters of purple flowers. "My grandmother loved them." Then I laughed.

"What?"

"Grandpa—he was not so keen on them. He said they smelled like a 'house of ill repute'".

"Is that all they argued about?"

"Pretty much."

"Good for them." As I buckled in next to him, Frank said, "Remember what you told me about that night delivery at the casino?"

"I remember. Have you solved the mystery?"

"Yes and no."

"Yes and no, how?"

"I mean, I know what was going on—but only because I read about it in the Ludington paper."

"Was it drugs?"

"Nothing that exciting. But it was fishy."

"Are you making me guess? I don't feel like games."

"Okay. The delivery was codfish. They were selling it in the restaurant as whitefish."

"So that's against the rules?"

"Against health department rules—but not enough to shut the place down. They just need to be more honest about what's on the menu." Frank handed me a flyer and said, "Take a look at this."

As we turned onto a side street, I read aloud from the pamphlet. "It says here that the 'Honoring our Elders Powwow' will be at the Shady Lane Campground; Admission is three bucks, and the Grand Entry is at two p.m."

"Then we should be right on time."

"Do you know what the grand entry is?"

"No, but I figure we should be there to find out. Also, that's when we're likely to find the most people."

I perused the flyer again. It listed the names of principal male and female dancers. "I see they've got a guy here who's come all the way from Arizona. That's a long trip. Do you think they get paid for this?"

"I doubt it very much. I think most folks do it for fun. They pack up and spend a month or two hitting a different powwow every weekend."

"Sounds like a good vacation, I guess."

"Here we are," Frank said. He made a right turn and drove through a gate where a man collected our admission fee and directed us to the guest parking lot.

"Take a left and follow the gravel road," said the man, who was wearing a ten-gallon hat. "After you park, just listen for the drums."

Following the directions, we drove past a camping area where I saw an assortment of motor homes, tents, travel trailers and quite a few traditional tepees. The guest parking lot was about half full. Frank found a spot that promised to offer shade later in the day.

As soon as I got out of the Blazer, I heard the steady beat of drums.

"Guess we just find the drums," he said.

Together we followed the sound, walking through a grove of maple and birch trees, until we emerged in a clearing where concession stands were arranged in a large semi-circle. Inside the semi-circle was a ring marked out by a dozen posts with rope strung between them. At the center of the ring were six men who sat in a circle while they pounded on a single large drum.

I could not see the drummers' faces but their age was reflected in their hair, some shiny black, some grey or white. Most of them had long hair and a couple of them wore braids. Blue jeans and tee shirts were the common attire, although one man stood out in a bright red shirt trimmed with blue ribbons.

Frank and I blended easily into the crowd, which included as many Caucasians as Indians. People were relaxed and smiled at us with no particular curiosity.

I pulled out my steno pad and started jotting notes. My reporter's estimate was that close to a hundred people were scattered around the site. Men, women and quite a few children wandered about talking and eating, checking out the jewelry, crafts, furs and books for sale.

I saw Jane Fillips from the tourist bureau who was there with her grandchildren, a boy and a girl. We spoke for a few minutes.

"I've never been to a powwow before," she said.

"Neither have I."

"The kids are loving it. I think it's a good event for the community."

"Did you help arrange it?"

She nodded. "My sister-in-law is Native American. I've been working with her for a few years to find a good site."

Frank came over and I introduced him to Jane. We all stopped talking when a voice came booming over the loudspeaker. I looked around for the source. On the far side of the dance area was a wooden stage, where a tall man was speaking into a microphone. Behind him were a dozen grey-hairs who sat in chairs under a canvas awning. A banner that read "Honoring our Elders" was spread across the front of the platform.

The speaker announced that the Grand Entry was under way and would begin with the Veterans Parade. He invited any veterans in the audience to join in.

Over the next ten minutes, every branch of the service was represented as participants walked the circle with drummers beating out the cadence. First came the flag bearers followed by men, and the occasional woman, in uniform, who were then joined by some veterans from the audience.

As I watched the spectacle, images from old western movies went flashing through my mind. Looking at the veterans, I said to Frank, "These people went to war for the country that oppressed them."

"True," said Frank. "But they are a warrior culture."

After the homage to veterans came the Women's Shawl Dance, where the women, many in dresses but some in jeans, moved slowly around the circle in shuffling steps making graceful arm motions to display their shawls.

Then came the war dance, not nearly as sedate, with a lot of jumping, whooping and hollering. The war dancers, all male, were decked out in fancy dress that included chest plates, fringed leather leggings, and elaborate feathered headpieces. The men were led out by the primary male dancer, who proved to be a striking man of about thirty with shiny black hair in two long braids. He moved with a precision which suggested that he had done this dance many times before.

When the war dance was over, Frank and I started checking out the concessions. That's when I saw Mary Simon whom I had interviewed the previous fall. She was working at a trailer that sold fry bread and corn cake.

"Let's get some fry bread," I said. "I'd like to talk to Mary."

Frank nodded and we started walking toward the fry bread stand which was emanating wonderful greasy odors. Suddenly he stopped short.

"It's my phone," he said. "I'd better take this." He walked a few steps away to answer the call. Curious, I waited but couldn't hear much. The conversation lasted about two minutes.

He ended the call, looked at me and sighed. "That was Benny. I really hate to say this but—I have to leave."

"Right now?"

"I'm afraid so. Sorry to ruin our day. What do you want to do?"

"Well—I really need to stick around and get something for the paper. Why don't you just go and leave me here?"

"Are you sure?"

"Sure, I'm sure. There's plenty of people here who would give me a ride home. In fact, I could probably walk. I don't think it's more than a mile or two."

"Okay then, sorry about this. I'll come over this evening—we'll have dinner somewhere."

Frank gave me a perfunctory hug before he turned and walked away. He never did say what Sheriff Benny wanted him for. All I knew for sure was that I was now on my own at the Cedar County Indian Powwow.

CHAPTER TWENTY-EIGHT

I watched Frank walk away until he disappeared into the shadows of the birch and maple trees. Then I turned back to the concession area and headed for the booth that was selling fry bread. But before I got there, I heard someone call my name. Turning around, I spotted our photographer, Kyle, replete with camera hanging on a multicolored strap around his neck.

"Hey there," he said as he covered the distance between us. "Marge told me you were going to be here, but she didn't say when."

"Hi Kyle. I've been here maybe an hour—just wandering around. Did you get any shots of the dancers?"

"Yes, and the drummers too. The men—the war dancers—are definitely the most photogenic."

"Aren't those quite the costumes? Sort of like the birds—the male of the species wears the brightest plumage."

"I got several shots of the head dancer—the one from out of state. You planning to interview him?"

"I will if I can find him."

"Okay, good. I've got to run. I'm shooting a wedding this evening for my cousin."

"Where's the wedding?"

"East Lansing."

"Then you'd better get going. Have fun."

"Thanks. I'm out of here." And with that, Kyle was gone.

By this time there was a line at the booth for fry bread but I didn't mind the wait. I got in line and talked to the woman in front of me, who was there with her two little boys.

"We've got a cottage on Lake Michigan," she said, "but the water's not warm enough for them to be in it all day long. I think this is really educational for them."

I agreed with her. We chatted about the fine weather and the coming art fair until it was my turn to buy fry bread. I gave my order to Mary, whose face was red and shiny with perspiration from standing over a deep fryer of bubbling oil. "I'm covering this for the paper," I said. "Do you have time to talk?"

"I'll make time," said Mary as her round face broke into a grin. "I'm ready for a break. Just come around the back. I'll be out in a few minutes."

I took my purchase and walked behind the concession trailer, where I found some folding chairs and a big umbrella. I sat down and took a big bite of the crisp, greasy fry bread. Mary joined me a minute later. In one hand, she held a red handkerchief she was using to mop her brow, and her other hand held a bottle of water.

"What can you tell me about these powwows?" I said when she was seated next to me. "Do they happen every summer?"

Mary took a drink before she answered. "I'm not sure when it all got started—but we've been doing this for at least six years. The thing was held over by White Cloud for a while, but then it started getting bigger and we needed more space for camping. This is the first time we've used this location."

"How do you like it here?" I laid my steno pad on the table and scribbled on it while I ate.

"I like it a lot. Because it's pretty quiet and there is shade in the campground. A nice place to spend a few days."

"Who works with you?" I said with a nod at the trailer.

"My mom, my brother and my aunt. Other relatives if we need them. We make enough to cover our expenses and not a whole lot more."

"So you're not doing this for the money?"

"Definitely not a money maker," she said with a laugh. "But for us, the whole thing is a big three-day party. We meet people from all over the country and a lot of the same ones come back every year."

"Can I use your name in the paper?"

"Oh, sure. No problem What else do you need to know?"

I finished my fry bread so I could focus on my writing while Mary and I continued to talk. After about ten minutes, I saw someone motioning from a doorway of the trailer. It was a woman who looked like an older version of Mary.

"Guess I'd better go help mom," she said.

"Sure, thanks for your time. Hey, I need to talk to the head male dancer—the flyer said he was from Arizona. Do you know where I could find him?"

"Shouldn't be too hard. The dancers are camped right over there." Mary pointed to a spot on the other side of the dance ring. "I talked with him last night. Just go on over and ask anyone you see for Norman Stone."

"Will do. Thanks again."

Mary got up to leave, then leaned over and said in a mock whisper, "We all think Norman's pretty hot."

"He did kind of look that way."

"So you be careful, Tracy."

"Hah! You too, Mary. You're the one who's camping here tonight."

"So's my husband, unfortunately."

Mary disappeared inside the trailer. I finished making notes and stowed the notepad in my denim bag. Then I stood, shouldered the bag, and set off in search of Norman Stone. The dance presentation seemed to be winding down. The announcer said there would be another Grand Entry at six p.m. and, a few minutes later, even the drummers took a break.

Following Mary's directions, I walked around to the far side of the dance circle and spoke to the first person I saw. He was a tall sixtyish man wearing a ten-gallon hat and tooled leather boots.

"I'm looking for Norman Stone," I said. "Can you tell me where to find him?"

The man looked me up and down for a long moment before he replied.

"You're not with law enforcement, are you?"

"Goodness no," I said, suddenly grateful that I didn't have Frank with me. "Okay, come on then."

The man turned on his heel and moved with a loping gait through the forest of trees and trailers and tents, while I struggled to keep up. He stopped in front of a canvas tent fronted by a fire pit that showed the remains of a recent fire. The pit was surrounded by half a dozen folding chairs and a whole lot of empty pop cans. My guide leaned down and spoke into the tent.

"Norman," he said, "you decent?"

"More or less," came the answer.

"Lady here wants to see you."

"I'll be right out."

"Okay girlie, you just wait here." Without saying goodbye, the man turned and walked away.

Minutes later, Norman Stone emerged through the low tent door and stood to greet me. The feathered headdress was gone and the leather leggings had been replaced by worn blue jeans. His feet were bare and he wore a faded tee shirt that said something about Wounded Knee. Up close and personal, Stone appeared to be on the far side of forty, but was still a fine looking man.

"Hi," he said softly. "I'm Norman."

We shook hands. "I'm Tracy Quinn. I write for the local paper and I just—." *was I really at a loss for words?* I cleared my throat. "If you don't mind, I just wanted to ask you a few questions. Our photographer said he had some pictures of you dancing so I, um, I just wanted to know a little more about you—have you been doing powwows all your life?"

"Oh, hell no. Have a seat."

"Thanks." I sank into a tattered chair.

"Want a drink?" He sat down on a wooden stool.

"Sure." Stone opened a cooler and peered inside. "Looks like Coke or root beer."

"Either one is fine."

"Sorry it's not very cold." He handed me a can of root beer and I popped it open.

I took out my steno pad, balanced it on my knee. "Did you grow up in Arizona?"

"Yes, I did." Norman opened his soda and took a long drink. "Near Flagstaff. Lived mainly but not always on the rez. Halfway between the two worlds. Didn't seem to fit in either one. Barely graduated from high school. Did a couple years in the army and then tried college at Arizona State."

I was scribbling fast to keep up with him.

Stone picked up a cloth tobacco pouch and a packet of rolling papers. He continued to talk while he extracted one of the papers, held it horizontal and poured a line of tobacco on it. I watched with fascination. Near as I could tell, he never dropped a shred of the tobacco as he licked one edge of the paper and proceeded to hand roll the cigarette.

"The Indian disease—that's alcohol—caught up with me and I got in trouble. Did some time in prison." He used his teeth to tighten the drawstring on the pouch, struck a match against a stone, and lit the cigarette.

"There was a group that came to the prison once a month and had meetings with us. Taught us about the Navaho code talkers and stuff like that. They kind of helped me feel better about being an Indian."

By now I was torn between writing and just wanting to listen. Norman Stone's story was making me realize how easy my life had been.

"So when I got out," he said, "I started to spend time with that bunch and that's when I started going to powwows. I learned the dances and got the regalia—that's what we call our fancy dress. I took some computer classes in prison so now I work in the Tribal office. But every summer I take a month and go on the powwow circuit. This is the second time I've been in Michigan." He paused, took a drag on his hand rolled cigarette. "Believe me, this is a good time of year to get out of Arizona."

After that our conversation drifted around—we talked about the Tony Hillerman novels, what life is like on the reservation, and how some clans have animal names and what each animal symbolizes. He told me he had been part of a group that went to South America in an effort to help the indigenous people there, who were fighting to keep their land.

"Okay," I said at last. "How much of this is okay to put in the paper? I mean—what about the prison stuff?"

"Sure, why not? It's part of my story. Might help someone else."

"Well, great," I said as I folded up my note pad. "You've given me plenty to write about—and think about too." I dropped my notebook into my bag and that's when I noticed the sketch that Frank had given me when we left my house.

I thought for a few seconds. Frank wasn't with me but I saw no harm in pursuing the issue on my own. I pulled the sketch out of my purse and showed it to Norman.

"Does this woman look like anyone you know?"

"Let me see."

I handed it over. He held the picture. First he glanced and then he stared at it while his eyes widened. "Well I'll be damned."

"You know her?"

"She looks like—it could maybe be—my Aunt Dalene."

I felt my heart leap in my chest. "Yes, her name is Dalene."

"She's my mother's sister. Mom said she was supposed to be in Michigan and maybe I would run into her while I was here. Why are you looking for her? Is she in trouble?"

CHAPTER TWENTY-NINE

This was going to be difficult. But I couldn't see any way around it.

"I'm sorry to tell you this, but it looks pretty certain that your aunt Dalene is dead."

Norman Stone took the news in silence. There was a nearly imperceptible jerk of his shoulders as he threw down the butt of his cigarette and ground it out with his heel. He looked down at the dirt.

"I'm really sorry." The words caught in my throat.

Now he looked straight at me, his eyes dry. "We figured something happened to her—my mother did anyway. "

He held the picture and stared at it some more. It was almost like he didn't want to ask the next question. "How did she die?"

"Unfortunately—she—um—she was murdered."

"Murdered." Another long pause. "How?"

"Strangled."

Still he was silent. No tears. I got the feeling that this was not the first time he had been touched by violent death.

"Do they know who did it?"

"That's what we're trying to find out," I said. "But everything has stalled because we didn't even know who she was." I explained that my boyfriend was a detective who was working the case. "What was her last name?"

"Fremont. Dalene Fremont."

"Frank will definitely want to talk with you," I said. "How long are you going to be here?"

"I was planning to leave tomorrow. But I can stay longer if it will help."

"I'll call Frank as soon as I get home and tell him to get over here and talk with you. When was the last time you saw her?"

He thought for a moment. "Last summer, over at Kingman. We got together at my cousin's house for a barbecue. I didn't stay very long because the guys get to drinking and, well—I try to stay away from that. But then, just before Christmas, I saw mom and she told me that Dalene had gone to Michigan. Not much explanation—just hopped on a Greyhound bus and took off."

"Any idea where she was going—or why?"

"It didn't make any sense. Mom said she talked like it had something to do with money."

"With money—how?"

"Like maybe she was going to get some money."

"Maybe she got the money and that's what got her killed," I said.

"You think?"

"Sorry. I'm just making wild guesses. But it's going to make a huge difference now that we know who she is. Are you willing to talk with Frank?"

"Of course. Any time. We've got another Grand Entry at six but that should be over before eight."

"I'll tell him everything you told me. And, if he's not here tonight, you can expect him in the morning."

Now I was anxious to get home and call Frank with the news. I said goodbye to Norman Stone and thanked him profusely. He walked with me to the road that led out of the campground and gave me an address so I could send him a copy of his story when it ran in the newspaper.

I welcomed the walk home because it gave me time to think. If Dalene had come to Michigan expecting something good, she had gotten exactly the opposite. Did she have money on her when she was killed?

Who had dug that shallow grave in the Manistee National Forest?

Who had drugged her and strangled her?

And why?

Shadows were beginning to lengthen when I turned onto Maple Street and knew I was only five blocks from home. Soon I saw the trees in my yard, the lilac bushes and finally the house. Then I was walking up the driveway and into the house.

I was glad I had been able to talk with Norman alone, but now I was eager to share the news with Frank. He hadn't told me what was so important that Benny had to pull him away from our afternoon together. But I was almost feeling like we had finally cracked the case.

At least we knew who she was.

I was feeling tired but happy as I walked up the steps to my porch, opened the front door and stepped into the foyer. But the minute I was inside, I stopped short, overcome by a feeling that something was wrong—almost as though someone else was in my house. I wondered if Ivy had dumped Steven on me after all.

I tried to tell myself I was just being paranoid. But then I heard a noise—it sounded like the closet door behind me was sliding open.

"What—?"

That was the only word I got out before a crackling pain exploded in the back of my head. With it came a blinding flash of light. As the light slowly faded, so did all of my questions, all of my thoughts, all of everything that made me Tracy Quinn. I struggled to stay conscious but lost the battle and slipped into darkness.

CHAPTER THIRTY

First there was the throbbing—persistent, repetitive waves of pain. The pain was like broken glass, like rusty nails, like pools of molten lead. For a while, I couldn't even figure out where it all was— definitely my head, but my shoulders were hurting too, and so were my ankles, my wrists, my knees, my hips.

I struggled to open my eyes—which felt like they were glued shut. Maybe they were. I thought I got my right eye open but saw nothing except blackness. I wondered if I was blind—the victim of a stroke, maybe?

Maybe I had died and this was the hereafter. If so, this was not at all what I had expected. *what had I done to deserve this purgatory of pain and darkness?*

But if this was the afterlife, would I be so aware of my body? Would I even have a body? Because now I was sure that I did. Along with the pain, I was feeling a miserable, damp chill that went to the marrow of my bones.

To test this body theory, I tried to move. But my arms felt paralyzed and I couldn't move either leg. I thought I could move my index fingers but, since I couldn't see them, maybe it was all my fevered imagination.

Finally I managed to turn my head and, when I did, felt something coarse scraping against my right cheek—as though I were lying on sand or dirt. That would explain why I felt like I had sand in my eyes. I probably did.

At this point I realized that my brain was working. At least part of it was working because I was thinking, posing questions. I tried to speak, but my tongue seemed stuck to the roof of my mouth. I worked it loose and tried to generate some saliva.

My thoughts flew in all directions. I remembered reading about a woman who had been in a coma for three years. When she woke up, still paralyzed, she was unable to let anyone know that she could hear people talking about her as though she were a vegetable.

was this to be my fate?

But that woman had awakened in a hospital. I knew that, wherever I might be, it was not a hospital. This place smelled of mildew, rust and old shoes. Which brought me to the questions of where, exactly, was I?

The pain had not gone away. It had not even noticeably decreased. But posing questions to my foggy brain gave me something else to focus on and that pushed the pain into a smaller area of my consciousness.

So—think. *where am I?*

And am I blind or—am I in a place so dark that there is nothing to see?

I was pretty sure that both of my eyes were open now. I blinked hard to test that theory. Still I saw nothing but darkness. But the darkness to the right was not as deep as the inky blackness to my left. So perhaps one eye was working—.

Just a little?

But what had brought me to this horrible place, lying in the dirt and unable to move anything except my eyelids and my head? I searched my memory banks. I remembered a sunny spring day and Frank coming to pick me up.

where the heck was Frank anyway?

He should be rescuing me from this hell I was in. But clearly but he wasn't doing that. So—back to trying to remember. I remembered eating fry bread at the powwow—and watching feathered dancers as they moved in the sunlight. Then I remembered talking to someone—that nice looking man called Norman something.

How had I gotten from there to here? Did Norman have anything to do with it?

Nothing made any sense. Now I could see a pale rectangle of light off to my right. But maybe the light was just an illusion.

I remembered walking home from the powwow—alone. Not sure why Frank wasn't with me. I remembered walking into my house—feeling a tinge of fear—just before pain crashed through my skull and the world was extinguished.

In a flash, I understood why I couldn't move my arms or my legs. It was not because I was paralyzed. The reason was that someone had knocked me out, tied me up and left me here to rot.

CHAPTER THIRTY-ONE

Oddly enough, it came as a relief when I gathered together enough scraps of memory to realize that I was not dead, I was not in a coma, and I was not crazy.

It was a relief to figure out that I had been assaulted and kidnapped.

I was not paralyzed, I was tied up. I moved my fingers, touched them with my thumbs. I turned my head, grinding more dirt into my scalp. So far, so good.

My brain was working a little better now.

I did my best to ignore the pounding in my head while I assessed what I knew about my situation. The person hiding in my closet had whacked me on the head, tied me up and left me lying on the dirt in this dank, frigid place.

But there was that rectangle of light off to my right, only a few inches above the level of my head.

I believed that the light was coming through a dirty, cobwebbed window. This suggested that I was in some kind of crawl space under an old building. And the window, though small, represented possible salvation—because it was made of glass.

But first I had to get close enough to the window to break it. I wiggled my toes and decided that I had shoes on. My feet would have to do the job.

The light was getting stronger. By now I had moved my fingers enough to feel that my wrists were secured with tape—and my ankles too. I rolled onto my back and bent my knees, the exertion setting off pain in my cramped muscles.

Then I used my shoulders and feet to scooch myself, an inch at a time, across the dirt, angling to get my feet closer to the window. I didn't rest until I was positioned at a right angle to the window and my feet were touching it.

My knees were bent so I straightened them out, kicking at the dirty glass. The maneuver didn't break anything but it did send pain knifing up my back. I tried again. This time the pain was worse—but the glass still didn't crack.

So I moved even closer. I bent my knees up even tighter and kicked as though I were aiming at whatever devil had bound me up and left me here to die. This time I was rewarded by the sound of shattering glass.

Now I had to move again. I wanted to get my hands on the broken glass. So I started scooting again, and the light that came in through the broken window suggested that dawn was breaking in the outside world.

I took a good look at my handiwork in order to plan my next move. Almost all of the broken glass had fallen on the far side of the window, but there were plenty of jagged shards left in the frame.

I kept that picture in my mind as I started to move again. Since my hands were trussed behind me, I needed to have my back to the window. When I finally got close enough, I moved my hands closer to the window frame, now edged with shards of broken glass.

I forced my bound hands into the frame of the broken window. I used my fingers to search for a sharp triangle of glass and, when I cut myself, I knew I had found it. I struggled to position my hands so the glass had a nice edge on the tape between my wrists.

Then I had to rest. My shoulders were burning from the effort, but my arms still had more work to do. After a minute, I started moving my bound hands up and down. Since I couldn't see any of it, I could only hope that the glass was sawing against the tape the way I had planned.

Minutes later, I had to rest again. The effort had so exhausted me that I was tempted to just give up, fall asleep and never wake up again. It would be so easy. All I had to do was close my eyes. And when they found my body—.

Nope. I forced my eyes open. I didn't know who had put me in this place, but I was determined that I wouldn't die here. If no one was coming to rescue me, I would just have to do it myself.

Back to working the tape against the glass. My hands were wet with blood. I thought about my mother, my grandmother, my grandpa—all of them long gone. Certainly they had done their best to help me grow up strong and smart and brave. They wouldn't want my life to end like this.

And that is when the tape gave way and my hands were free.

Slowly I brought my hands around to the front of my body. There was just enough light to see now, and the sight of my bloody hands and my wrists wrapped with duct tape confirmed everything I had been imagining. I almost cried with relief as I cautiously moved my hands to my face, grateful to have the use of those eight marvelous fingers and wonderful opposable thumbs.

But my work wasn't finished. My feet were still bound together and, if I wanted to get out of this place, I had to be able to walk.

I managed to peel off some pieces of the tape and stuck them to the inside of my right hand. Using the tape as protection, I broke off a shard of glass from the window frame. The tape didn't protect me as much as it should have and I managed to cut my thumb. But now I had a tool.

I bent down and started cutting away at the tape that bound my ankles together. This endeavor was made easier by the fact that I could see what I was doing. Within minutes the tape ripped apart and my ankles were free.

I didn't waste any time celebrating. I had to get out of this prison. The window was too small to serve as an exit—I needed to find another way out.

I tried to stand but my head quickly bumped the ceiling, which seemed to be about three feet above the dirt I was lying on. But the dirt floor was not level. It was on an slant, getting lower away from the window. So I rolled and scooted down the incline, until my feet hit what felt like a concrete floor. With both feet on the floor and my cold butt in the dirt, I struggled to stand up.

This made me so dizzy that I almost collapsed. I reached out to steady myself and felt a stone wall. I kept one hand on the wall while I continued to straighten up. The space was just deep enough to let me stand. With one hand against the wall, I inched forward with tiny, shuffling steps.

Once again, I was in nearly complete blackness. When my feet bumped against a cement barrier, I was afraid that I had hit another wall. But, on further exploration, the cement turned out to be the first of a series of steps. I struggled up four steps, until my head banged on wood. Damn! If this had once been an exit, it was now barricaded. Then I saw a sliver of light filtering through the dusty air.

Encouraged by that splinter of light, I reached over my head and pushed upward. The boards above me creaked and groaned and resisted. I stepped higher and put my back into the task until finally the wooden panel gave one last screech and flew upward. I had just opened a trapdoor.

Daylight opened up around me. Emerging slowly into the blessed fresh air, I heard the cry of sea gulls, the susurration of waves.

I looked around and saw a forest of charred timbers. I was standing in a field of rubble—cracked cement, broken bricks and shattered glass. The scene looked like a war torn city after a bombing raid.

That's when I realized where I was.

And I had a pretty good idea who had put me there.

CHAPTER THIRTY-TWO

My escape from the dungeon left me weak as a lamb.

Looking down, I saw that my hands were bleeding and my jeans were soaked with blood. I was shivering, either from cold or from shock, maybe both. I shook my head, trying to clear away the spots that were crowding my field of vision. Dizzy, I sank down onto a chunk of concrete and took in a deep breath of the clean air.

Deep breath in and hold—blow out slowly—breathe in—breathe out.

I needed help, that was for sure.

There was the lake and there was the beach, but what I needed right now was people. I looked away from the lake and saw a hedge of cedar trees with a light peeking through it. The light seemed to be part of a house. So I got up and started walking. I stumbled over stones and burned grass, through the cedar hedge and right across somebody's flower bed.

The house was yellow with lots of windows.

I knocked on the door. There was no response.

I saw a button which might have been a door bell and pushed it. Still nothing happened. Close to tears, I started pounding.

The door flew open and revealed a startled looking man in a green bathrobe.

The poor man just stood and stared—as though he were looking at some kind of dirty, bleeding monster with matted hair and tape hanging from every appendage. Because that's exactly what I was.

"What going on?" said a woman's voice. Seconds later, Joyce Meeker appeared beside her husband. She took one look at the apparition in her doorway and said, "My god, Fred, let her in. It's Tracy Quinn."

That sounded like an invitation so I stumbled through the door.

Moving quickly to catch me before I fell, Joyce and Fred each took one of my arms. They led me into their living room and let me collapse on a sofa. I saw Fred pick up a telephone and felt a sweet sense of relief as Joyce laid a blanket over me. That's when my body and brain agreed that it would be okay to pass out again.

So I closed my eyes and let it happen.

CHAPTER THIRTY-THREE

When I woke up, I expected to be in Fred and Joyce Meekers' house.

But no, this place was different. Off to my right I saw a pole holding a plastic bag with a tube snaking down to my arm. So it was an IV. And I was in a hospital.

Voices floated on the air.

"Looks like she's waking up."

"Better call the director—."

"You sure?"

"Yes. She said she absolutely wanted to know—. "

I closed my eyes. Probably dozed off again—until I felt somebody touching my hand.

"Tracy. Tracy, can you hear me?"

I opened my eyes and saw a wonderful sight. It was my best friend Jewell and she looked like an angel.

"Hi Jew—," I said, but my words came out like a croak.

"Thirsty?"

I nodded. Jewell reached for a glass and fed me a spoonful of ice. My parched mouth soaked up the moisture.

Jewell pulled a chair up beside my bed. She sat down and fed me more ice until I was finally able to speak.

"What happened?" I said

"That's what we're trying to figure out. But the important thing is that you're safe. Hope I didn't hurt your hand." She looked down at my bandaged wrist and palm.

"My hand's okay, it's my head doesn't feel too good." I reached up to check the back of my skull. My fingers found a bandage, then a bristly patch of hair.

"Sorry, but we had to shave part of your head," she said as I continued to explore the spot with my fingers. "You have twelve stitches up there—and head wounds tend to bleed a lot. Your hair was all matted with blood—and full of dirt and coal dust."

"Did I lose a lot of blood?"

"Quite a lot. We gave you a transfusion."

I stared at her, with so many questions racing through my mind that I hardly knew where to begin. So I started with a simple one. "Jewell, why are you working on Sunday?"

"Surprise Tracy—it's Monday."

"Oh crap. Looks like I lost a day somewhere."

"What can you remember?"

"I remember the powwow was on Saturday and then—."

Jewell looked away from me to a figure in the doorway. "There's somebody here to see you," she said as she patted my hand and moved away.

The figure in the doorway proved to be Frank Kolowsky. He and Jewell exchanged a few whispers before he came into the room and sat in the chair by my bed.

"Hey Tracy," he said gently. "How's it going?"

"Not my best day." I struggled to return Frank's smile. "I must look a fright."

"You look good to me."

"Sure, with my head shaved and wearing this gorgeous white shirt."

"You had us worried. We had the whole department out looking for you."

"That's flattering, I guess. But I had to rescue myself."

"I am sorry about that."

"When did you know I was missing?"

"Saturday evening. Remember we were supposed to get together?"

"Right. Guess I stood you up."

"When I didn't find you at home, I went back to the campground and looked for you there. When I didn't find you there, I started calling. I called everyone I could think of—even Ivy. Did you even get home after the powwow?"

"Just barely. I walked home but, the minute I got in the house, somebody whacked me on the head." I paused, trying to remember. "Have you caught the guy who did this?"

"Do you know who it was?"

"Not sure, but my guess is Clint Pomeroy. Since I was stashed in the basement of his burned-out building."

"You guessed right."

"What I don't understand is why—."

"Pomeroy kidnapped you to buy himself some time. He figured if we were busy looking for you, he could get out of the country before we arrested him."

"Arrested him—for what?"

"For the murder of Dalene Fremont."

That made sense in a way, but it also didn't make any sense. That's when Frank's cell phone buzzed. He looked at it and said, "I'd better take this." He stepped out of my room and was gone about two minutes.

When he came back in, he said, "Sorry but I've gotta go. You get some rest." He kissed me on the forehead and was gone.

Now I really had a lot of questions. But I forgot all of them when the nurse gave me a pain shot that put me to sleep and gave me lovely dreams. I awakened when a doctor with bright blue eyes came to check me out. He looked at my head wound, shone a flashlight in my eyes, and asked me if I knew the name of the president and what year it was. I answered his questions—correctly I believe—and closed my eyes.

Later a nurse took came to take the IV out of my arm. She asked me if I wanted to get up to the bathroom and I said I'd give it a try. We managed that excursion but, when I got back to bed, I was so tired that I dozed off again.

When I woke up, Jewell was beside me. "I see you've been on your feet," she said. "How do you feel?"

"Better—a lot better."

"Good. Doctor said if your vitals are stable you can go home tomorrow. I'll bring some clothes for you to wear."

"Okay, but tell me—why did Frank run out of here like that? Did I miss something?"

"I don't know for sure. But I would guess it had something to do with Clint Pomeroy."

Jewell wasn't able to tell me anything more so I had to be satisfied with the information I had. A girl in a blue uniform brought me a supper tray. I ate some broth and orange jello. For a while I tried to figure things out, but my brain got so tired that I gave up and fell asleep. In the morning, I had a poached egg and toast for breakfast. And coffee—what a treat.

Doctor Blue Eyes checked me over again and told me I was okay to go. A nurse's aide brought in clothes and helped me get dressed. She presented the discharge papers for me to sign and, when I looked up, Frank was waiting to take me home.

Jewell came to see us off.

"Frank has agreed to keep an eye on you for the next couple of days," she said. Then she crooked a finger at him. He came closer and she whispered, "Remember, no hanky panky."

"Yes, ma'am," he said. It was the first time I had seen Frank blush.

I thanked Jewell and everybody within sight. The aide put me in a wheelchair, pushed me down a long hallway and out into the sunshine. The world had never looked so good.

The Blazer was waiting and Frank helped me climb in.

"Okay," I said. "Now tell me about Clint Pomeroy."

CHAPTER THIRTY-FOUR

"Clint Pomeroy is in the Kent County jail," said Frank. "The state police picked him up at the Grand Rapids airport as he was about to board a plane for Chicago—with connections to Belize."

"So he was definitely on his way out of the country."

"No doubt about that."

"Okay. Let me get this straight. You said he knocked me out and put me in that cellar—."

"The charge will be assault and kidnapping."

"Okay. Clint Pomeroy kidnapped me because you were coming after him for killing Dalene?"

"That's right."

"So how did you get on to him? I mean, we kept poking around the casino—no one had even considered him as the killer."

Frank maneuvered out of the hospital parking lot and onto the road before he answered. "It was Joel Dukes who put us on to him."

"Joel? How does he come into this?"

"Remember Saturday when we were at the powwow?"

"Right."

"I took a call from Sheriff Benny."

"I remember. What was so important that you had to leave?"

"Benny called me because Joel Dukes had just contacted him. Joel said he had information he wanted to share. So I drove to Stanton to meet with Joel and the sheriff."

"What did Joel have to tell you?"

"He told us he was handling the Pomeroy estate. Charles Pomeroy died over two years ago, but there was no payout because two heirs were named in the will. One of them was his son, Clint and the other was a daughter. Despite his best efforts, Joel had not been able to locate the daughter."

"Interesting." I thought back to the argument I had witnessed at the yacht club between Joel Dukes and Clint Pomeroy.

"Joel reads the papers so he knew, of course, about the body we had found in the national forest. But he never made any connection—at least, not until Pomeroy got more demanding and irrational about needing the money."

"I remember now. At the yacht club he said to Joel, 'she could be dead for all we know.'"

"So Joel started thinking that maybe, just maybe, the woman in the woods was the missing sister. And he shared his suspicion with Benny and me."

"But—this woman was—Indian."

"I should have said half-sister. Apparently Charles fathered this child back when he was in college in Flagstaff. He never married the mother, but they kept in some kind of contact. And when he died, he wanted to leave his daughter a share of his estate."

"Oh, how sad. Instead of helping her, he got her killed."

"Unfortunately. After talking with Joel, Sheriff Benny and I decided to visit Pomeroy and ask him some questions. We went to his cottage and knocked on all the doors—but everything was locked and we got no answer."

"Was his car there?"

"Garage was locked too."

"Couldn't you just break down a door?"

"Well no. Not without a warrant."

"It's not like television?"

"Almost never. So Benny and I left the cottage. We went back to Stanton to work on getting a warrant. It took us most of the afternoon to reach the judge because he was out of town for the weekend. Judge Veenstra said he would come back Sunday to help us out. So that's when I drove over to your place."

"Guess I was already gone—."

"Yes. Because Clint Pomeroy had been inside his cottage when Benny and I came looking for him. That's when he knew we were on to him—so he hatched his getaway plan."

"This must have happened awfully fast."

"He acted quickly. Booked a flight and then kidnapped you. Do you remember what time you got home?"

"I don't know. Maybe five-thirty. "

"I got to your place about seven."

"I suppose by that time I was in the cellar. I wonder why it took me so long to wake up?"

"Looks like he gave you some Xanax."

"Really? I don't remember that."

"He could have injected it."

"That seems to be his drug of choice."

"Yes, he had a prescription for it."

"I'm lucky he didn't kill me," I said, thinking of the body in the forest.

"On Sunday, we widened the search for you. But we also got into Pomeroy's house, checked his computer, and found that he had booked a flight for Monday. So we knew what time he would be at the airport to catch his flight. Benny talked to the State Police, told them he was a murder suspect, and they promised to pick him up at the airport."

"So did they?"

"Yes they did. And welcome home," Frank said as we pulled into my driveway. "I'm sorry you had to go through that ordeal in the coal cellar. In hindsight, we should have thought to look there—but the fact is that we hadn't made a strong connection between your disappearance and the Pomeroy case."

"Do you think you would have looked there eventually?"

"Oh, of course."

"Right—you would have found my body."

"So maybe it's dangerous to have me in your life. Do you want to dump me?"

"Never."

Frank helped me out of the Blazer and kept an arm around me as we walked up the steps and across the porch. He paused to open my front door and said, "Okay now, here we go."

And before I knew what was happening, he picked me up and carried me inside.

CHAPTER THIRTY-FIVE

On a sunny afternoon about two weeks later, Frank and I drove out to the Indian cemetery in Elbridge Township. The body we had found in the woods was going to be buried again, this time in a pine box and with an appropriate ceremony.

We didn't know exactly who would be there and were surprised to find more than thirty people waiting at the graveside. Most were standing, but a few of the elders were seated in folding chairs. Mary Simon was there and so was Norman Stone.

When she saw me, Mary came over and said, "I'm glad you two could come. We're just waiting for Mickey Two Trees."

Minutes later a man with wrinkled skin the color of bronze came walking over a little rise. He moved slowly, leaning heavily on his walking stick, a polished oak limb with irregular bumps and whorls.

"That's him," said Mary.

Mickey was dressed in a leather shirt and jeans with a single feather in his hair. He carried a leather bag. The waiting group fell back, making room for him at the head of the grave.

Mickey reached into his bag and extracted a bunch of sweetgrass. Then he struck a match and lighted the bundle. As the smoke rose, he spread it around with a fan of eagle feathers and began to chant. He continued to chant as he slowly circled the grave.

When the circle was complete, he stopped and bowed to each of the four directions. Norman Stone stepped up beside him and sprinkled some tobacco on the ground. Then everybody sang together, a song that sounded like "Amazing Grace", but was in a different language.

Afterward there was food in the basement of the church—wild rice, potato salad, hot dogs, and several kinds of pie. Norman Stone came over and sat with me and Frank.

"Thank you for finding my aunt," he said. "Without you two, we would never have known what happened to her."

"It's good that you could have this service for her," said Frank.

"It is," he said. "It's wonderful. None of these people knew her but, as soon as they heard the story, they found enough money to give her a burial."

"Mary told me that you plan to have a headstone," I said.

"That's my project for the coming year," Norman said with a smile, "to save enough money for a headstone. Next spring I'll bring my mother out here with me so she can say goodbye to her sister."

"That's good," I said. "It means you will be coming back to Michigan."

"I'm starting to like Michigan," said Norman. "And now I will always have a reason to come back."

THE END

EPILOGUE

Almost a month later, the stitches were out of my scalp but I still had a patch of hair that was only half an inch long. I had taken to wearing hats much of the time and my friends gave me so many of them that I had an extensive collection. I was wearing a cute straw number with flowers on the brim as Frank and I sat on a dune overlooking Lake Michigan.

"I've been thinking," he said.

"What about?"

"When you went missing, I realized—well—I realized that you're pretty important to me."

"Good. You're important to me too."

"So I was wondering." He leaned over and brushed some sand from my cheek. "Would you want to consider, um, getting married?"

He must have heard me gasp because he amended the proposal.

"I mean, not right away. Just sometime."

My failed first marriage flashed before my eyes. I still couldn't answer, so Frank amended the proposal again.

"I mean, we could be engaged."

"Okay," I said at last. "We could be engaged."

After that Frank and I stayed on the dune, looking out over the lake and not talking very much. We watched the sky change from orange to blaze red and finally shade into deep purple as the sun slipped into the lake.

And still we lingered—quiet and contented—sitting on the warm sand and wrapped in the darkness of a Midsummer's Eve.